FELLED IN LITTLE LEAF CREEK

A LITTLE LEAF CREEK COZY MYSTERY
BOOK SEVENTEEN

CINDY BELL

ISBN: 9798365952461

Cassie Alberta tightened the laces of her boots and tied a strong knot. A buzz of excitement crackled through the air all around her. She smiled as she listened to the words exchanged above her head.

"I want that tree." Stephanie Vail crossed her arms as she looked at her older brother.

"But who gets it will be determined by who wins, right?" Sebastian Vail glanced over at Cassie as she straightened up, and his smile widened. "And since I have Cassie on my team, I'm pretty sure that we're going to win."

"No way." Stephanie pursed her lips. "I'm great at scavenger hunts. I'll be done in the blink of an eye."

"I'm not so sure about that." Cassie looked over the list that a woman who looked about twenty handed to her. "There are quite a few items on here."

"And they're all different." The young woman waved Stephanie away as she tried to get a look at Cassie's list. "Here, this one is for you." She held out another list to Stephanie.

"Wait, all of us have a different list?" Stephanie glanced at hers. "That makes things harder."

"Exactly, it means that you can't follow each other around the farm. You have to look for your own items. Here you are." She passed a list to Tessa Watters as she stepped closer to the group. "I think this is such a fun idea. You will all have a great time, and the trees on this farm are spectacular. And it's for a good cause. The scavenger hunt is to raise money for a children's charity, to help families that can't afford gifts for Christmas. Even if you don't happen to win a tree, I'm sure you'll want to buy one to take home with you."

"You make a pretty good saleswoman." Tessa looked at her. "But I don't think I know you, and I know just about everyone in this town. This is Nancy's farm, isn't it?"

"Yes, it is. But I'm helping her out. My name is

Nina." She smiled at Tessa. "And I've heard all about you."

"You have?" Tessa raised her eyebrows. "I'm not sure if that's a good thing."

"I've heard quite a few complaints about a retired police detective being part of the scavenger hunt." Nina's smile widened. "I believe people think you will have an unfair advantage."

"Well, I guess we'll just have to prove them right." Mark Collingswood, dressed in a bright green suit and coat, with a Christmas ornament on his tie, draped his arm around Tessa's shoulders. "With the two of us working together, no one else stands a chance."

"What am I going to do with a Christmas tree?" Tessa shrugged his arm off, then looked back at Nina. "So, you're a new employee of Nancy's, then?"

"Not exactly." Nina swallowed hard, then glanced at another group gathered together. "I should keep handing these out. The hunt will be starting soon. Good luck to all of you!"

"Thank you. No matter what, I'm sure we're all going to have a blast." Cassie grinned as she looped her arm through Sebastian's. "It's all about the experience."

"Cassie! Tessa!" Mirabel Light yelled from the parking lot as she and Detective Oliver Graham hurried toward them through the snow-covered ground. "Are we too late?"

"No, it hasn't started, yet. That young lady over there, Nina, is handing out lists." Tessa pointed her out.

"I'll go grab us one." Oliver squeezed Mirabel's shoulder, then walked over to Nina.

"So you've met her?" Mirabel leaned close to Cassie and Tessa and lowered her voice. "She's the talk of the whole town."

"What do you mean?" Cassie asked. "What could people possibly have to say about her? She seems nice enough."

"You haven't heard?" Mirabel looked between them. "I don't like to gossip, but it's all around town, so you'll hear soon enough. Nina is Nancy's daughter."

"What?" Tessa shook her head. "Nancy doesn't have a daughter. She's never had any children."

"That's what most of us thought." Mirabel crossed her arms as she smiled. "But our little town has more secrets than it has residents. Apparently, Nancy had a secret pregnancy and gave the baby up for adoption. Nina recently showed up to reunite with her mother. Now, the whole town is out here for the scavenger hunt, more to get a good look at Nancy and Nina than for charity, or to win a Christmas tree. Although, Ollie and I are determined to get one. If we don't win one, we'll just buy one. We want to make Maisy's Christmas with us special. June will be joining us, and we're all looking forward to it."

Mirabel had become Maisy's guardian when June, Maisy's grandmother, could no longer take care of the young teen.

"That's wonderful." Cassie bit into her bottom lip. She'd come to the tree farm to get a tree and introduce Sebastian to a few of the family traditions she had during childhood, which she had left behind during her life of luxury, but now she felt herself rooting as much for her friends to win.

"It looks like they're getting ready to start." Stephanie pointed toward a small group of women who stood at the front of the crowd.

Cassie recognized them from when they had occasionally come into the diner, but she had never really spoken to any of them.

"That's Nancy, and her sister Sally." Tessa squinted and took a step forward. "And that's Marie, Nancy's best friend." She sighed as she shook her head. "Nina's really Nancy's daughter? I don't see the resemblance."

"She probably takes after her father." Mirabel shrugged. "Who remains a complete mystery. Though, if the gossips in this town have anything to say about it, we'll know who it is by the end of the day."

"Maybe it's best to leave it alone." Tessa's voice softened. "Nancy must have had a good reason to keep it all a secret."

"This is a first." Mark looked into Tessa's eyes. "I didn't think I'd ever see the day when you would want to leave a mystery a mystery."

"Some secrets have a purpose." Tessa looked back at Nancy. "She's lived a good life, and now she has a chance to share that with her daughter. That's resolved enough for me."

"All right, everyone!" Nancy waved her gloved hands through the air. "You will have exactly one hour to find as many things as you can on your list. When you hear the bells ring, that means you're done, and you must return your list to one of us within five minutes, or you will be disqualified. Good luck, and Merry Christmas!" She grinned as the crowd began to rush forward to hunt through the trees.

A man in the crowd strode straight toward Nancy, caught her by the arm, and steered her away from the rest of the group. Cassie recognized him from serving him at the diner a couple of times. She knew his name was Kevin. She hadn't really spoken to him aside from the usual pleasantries, but he seemed friendly.

"Let's go!" Sebastian grabbed Cassie's hand and tugged her toward the trees. "Stephanie already has a head start."

Oliver and Mirabel took off in another direction.

Cassie's gaze lingered on Kevin and Nancy for a moment longer as she sensed the tension in their interaction. Another tug from Sebastian drew her attention back to him.

"Yes, let's go!" She grinned. "Although, I don't know if we stand a chance with Tessa and Mark in the competition."

"I think you might be overestimating their ability to work as a team." Sebastian chuckled as he pointed to the pair squabbling over which way to go. He squeezed Cassie's hand and smiled. "Whether or not we win, I'll never doubt what a great team we make."

Cassie hugged him.

"Agreed."

A cool breeze ruffled the hair off the back of her neck, sending a chill down her spine. She hugged Sebastian a little tighter, then followed his lead into the trees. As the rest of the crowd began searching, she heard shouts and laughter all around her. A rush of Christmas spirit filled her. Things had certainly changed in her life. She'd gone from a youth, when her family was struggling for money, to a wealthy man's wife, to his widow, and now she clung to the hand of a man she never expected to meet but couldn't imagine living without. She couldn't be happier.

CHAPTER 2

Tessa zipped her coat up to her neck and did her best to ignore the cold air. It had taken quite a lot of convincing to get her to join in on the scavenger hunt, when she could have been happily nestled in her favorite chair in her nice warm house.

"Let's go, then." Mark grinned. "We can't win, if we don't try."

"You're welcome to try as hard as you'd like." Tessa matched his pace despite the slight limp in her gait. She had been shot when she was a detective and was protecting Oliver. "I'm just here to keep an eye on things."

"Always on the job?" Mark glanced over at her. "Don't you ever just take a day off and relax?"

"I am relaxed. I'm perfectly relaxed." Tessa took a deep breath, then let it out slowly. "Let's just get this over with." She eyed a giant wreath propped up by tall metal poles at the center of the rows of trees that branched off in all directions. "Someone spent a pretty penny on that monstrosity."

"It's nice, though." Mark looked it over, then met her eyes. "I think I spy some mistletoe."

"The only toe you're going to spy is mine swinging right toward your nose, if you keep up that nonsense." Tessa huffed as she brushed past him.

"You don't scare me, Tessa." Mark chuckled as he followed after her.

She looked over her shoulder and straight into his eyes.

"Yes, I do." She continued down the path. The sound of his footsteps against the snow and frozen leaf litter alerted her to his company. Otherwise, he remained silent.

Tessa looked down at the list in her hand, then pursed her lips.

"These first few are easy. All we have to do is snap pictures of what we see." She slowed down to let him catch up. "It might be faster if we split up."

"I'd rather stick together."

"Got the first item." Tessa pointed out a tree

with strong branches tipped with deep-green needles. "That's our Fraser fir."

"There are hundreds of them." Mark smiled as he pulled out his phone and snapped a picture. "Hey, how about a selfie?" He wrapped his arm around her shoulders and leaned his head toward hers as he raised the camera in the air.

"Do you want a broken phone?" Tessa swatted at his hand.

"Hey! This wasn't cheap, you know." Mark swung the phone away from her before she could knock it out of his hand.

"Then don't wave it in my face." Tessa looked back down at the list.

"You know, Tessa, if you spent a little less time pretending to be so angry, you might actually find that you're enjoying yourself." Mark laughed.

"You invited yourself, remember?" Tessa looked up at him. "No one is forcing you to be here."

"Impossible, you're just impossible." Mark turned away from her.

"No, this list is impossible. This whole thing is a scam."

"A scam?" Mark glanced back over at her. "What do you mean?"

"The next item is a Japanese maple tree leaf. I

have not seen one Japanese maple on this farm ever, and I've been coming here for years." Tessa held the list out to him. "This was a total waste of time. No one is going to be able to win that tree, if they put something like this on everyone's list."

"Hold on now. Maybe we shouldn't give up so easily." Mark took the list from her and studied it before he looked up at her again. "Even when things seem impossible, there's usually a way to make it work."

"Okay, then tell me how we're going to get a picture of a leaf from a tree that doesn't grow on this farm." Tessa shook her head. "I'm not sure that mystery has a solution."

"We'll figure it out. We just have to put our heads together." Mark held out his hand to her. "Teamwork?"

"Fine." Tessa gave his hand a quick shake. "If only to prove to you that some things are definitely impossible."

Mark smiled, then looked around. "Let's look. Maybe there are some Japanese maples around."

"Maybe, but I doubt it." As Tessa stepped forward, a smooth Southern accent caught her attention.

"Cassie, it has to be this one. I'm sure of it."

"It isn't the same pine cone that's on the list. See, this is what it should look like?" Cassie replied.

Tessa peered through the thin line of trees that separated the paths and watched as Cassie held up her phone to show something to Sebastian.

"Fine. I guess you're right, as usual." He laughed.

"Have you two had enough of this impossible scavenger hunt, yet?" Tessa stepped toward them. "I just told Mark, it's rigged. No one is going to win."

"Oh, we're going to win." Sebastian smiled. "I'm getting Cassie that tree."

"I don't even need to win a tree. I can just get another one," Cassie said.

"Well, you're going to get that one. I want to win. Let's find that pine cone." Sebastian took her hand.

"Oh look, there's Ollie up ahead." Cassie tipped her head toward Oliver and Mirabel huddled together. "Maybe he has some tips about where to find those pine cones."

"I can figure it out." Sebastian stared down at the list. "Just give me a minute."

"Absolutely. I know you will." Cassie started to take his hand when Oliver's sharp voice carried across the distance between them.

"What are you doing here? I should take you down to the station right now!"

Cassie watched Oliver lunge toward a man a few feet away from him.

The man spun around and held up his hands. "Easy, copper!" He chuckled. "I didn't do anything wrong."

"No? I heard about you going out to those properties and chopping down those trees to sell for firewood. It's illegal you know? You trespassed, and you stole from those families." Oliver took another step toward the man as Mirabel hovered close to him.

"Prove it!" The taller man smirked as he stared at Oliver. "If you could, I wouldn't be standing here, would I?"

"I will." Oliver crossed the last of the distance between them. "Don't you think for a second that I won't make sure that you're behind bars for what you did, Devon. I might not have the proof right now, but I will get it. You can count on that."

"Oh wow, terrifying." Devon smirked as he lowered his hands. "I guess it's easy to be that tough when you've got a gun on your hip, huh?"

"You need to go. You have no business being

here." Oliver pointed in the direction of the driveway.

"Don't I? It's a public event." Devon scowled. "These coppers, they just don't know how to be decent human beings, do they?" He laughed as he turned and walked off.

"What was that all about?" Cassie watched him walk away.

"That guy is bad news. He's known for illegal tree lopping on protected land, trespassing, and stealing trees for firewood. Spotting him on a Christmas tree farm makes me pretty suspicious." Oliver shook his head. "Unfortunately, I don't have enough proof that he's been active in this area to arrest him."

"Come on, Ollie, forget about Devon." Mirabel touched his arm. "You're supposed to be off duty today, remember? You promised we would spend the whole day together. We're not even finished the scavenger hunt."

"Okay," Oliver said.

"I think we should go home." Tessa looked at Mark. "It's freezing."

"There's no rush, is there? Can't we finish the hunt first?" Mark asked.

"The impossible hunt, you mean? We can

wander around here all day. We're never going to find that leaf on this farm." Tessa gestured around her.

Suddenly, Mark smiled.

"I know where it is!" Mark snapped his fingers as his eyes gleamed. "Tessa, follow me!"

"Okay, let's see." Tessa glanced at Cassie. "Why don't you join us and see if he's right?"

"Sure." Cassie grinned. "I don't mind tagging along. Sebastian and I are stumped anyway."

"I'm not stumped. We'll find everything." Sebastian stared down at the list in his hand as he trailed behind them.

"Aha! Here it is!" Mark grinned as they emerged where the large wreath stood. "If it can't be real, then it must be artificial! I bet there's a maple leaf somewhere on this wreath."

"Okay." Tessa took a slow breath. "I'll admit it. I'm impressed."

"Wait until I find it, then you'll really be impressed." Mark began peering at the different leaves on the wreath, then froze. "What's this?"

"Is something wrong?" Tessa stepped closer to him.

Cassie noticed the tension in Tessa's voice and looked toward the wreath as well.

Mark ran his finger across a white cloth petal, then looked up at them both.

"I think it's blood."

"Blood?" Tessa looked around his shoulder at the petal.

"What did you say?" Sebastian looked up from his list, then gasped. "Cassie, watch out!"

Cassie drew back before she could finish her next step, then looked down at the ground. Her stomach twisted at the sight of the dark-red snow stretching out from behind the large wreath.

"That's definitely blood." Tessa stared at the snow as Cassie gasped. "Everyone, stand back." Tessa's tone shifted from curious to authoritative. "Someone must be hurt." She peeked around the side of the wreath. Her shoulders slumped. "Or dead!"

Cassie followed her line of sight to a woman's body strewn across the ground. The ax lying beside her, and the pool of blood around her head, made it clear that she was dead. Murdered!

CHAPTER 3

"Oliver!" Tessa shouted his name as she crouched down beside the body. "Get over here!"

"Who is it?" Mark peered down at the body. "Can you tell?"

"It's Nancy." Tessa looked up as Oliver ran toward them. "I think this scavenger hunt is over."

"You need to get back." Oliver gestured with his hands as they moved a few steps back. "Mirabel, keep everyone back!" he shouted over his shoulder, then turned back to the body on the ground. "I'll call for backup." He looked around the area. "Is that an ax?"

"Yes, yes it is." Tessa followed his line of sight.

"I'll do my best to keep everyone back." Mark started toward a few curious onlookers.

"I'll help." Sebastian followed after him.

Cassie watched as Oliver crouched down and studied the wound on the back of Nancy's head.

"Who would do something like this?" Cassie met Tessa's eyes.

"That's the question, isn't it?" Tessa skimmed the crowd that had begun to grow.

"We'll find out soon enough, I guess." Cassie looked around as well.

Oliver stood up from the body and walked over to Tessa and Cassie.

"Did you see anyone nearby when you came toward the wreath?"

"No, nobody." Tessa glanced over at Cassie.

Mark walked over to them with an officer beside him.

"As you requested, some officers are getting the crowd under control. They're evacuating everyone back toward the main barn and the parking lot and taking statements." The officer stopped in front of Oliver.

"Thank you. Can you help rope off the crime scene, please?" Oliver watched as the officer nodded and walked off, then he looked back at Mark. "Did you see anyone around the area before you found the body?"

"No, just Sebastian and Cassie." Mark glanced at Tessa. "They walked over to the wreath with us."

"Maybe you heard someone walk past, or maybe a voice? Maybe people arguing?" Oliver squinted at him. "It might help us pin down a timeline for what happened. Maybe you heard someone running away or spotted someone through the trees?"

"No, nothing," Mark said.

"You didn't see or hear anyone? Maybe Nancy? She had to get there somehow." Oliver looked between them.

"No," Tessa said as Mark shook his head.

"And you were together the whole time?" Oliver shifted his gaze back to Tessa. "Neither of you went off on your own?"

"No, we were together." Tessa looked around trying to take in as much of the scene as possible.

"I was with Sebastian the whole time." Cassie took a deep breath as commotion swirled around her. It was easy to be distracted by the flurry of movement. She tried to focus, determined to see if there were any clues.

"Okay, we need to clear the area." Oliver

gestured for them to move farther back as an officer started putting police tape around the crime scene.

"We need to help find out who did this." Tessa looked over at Cassie as they walked away.

Cassie nodded. Like Tessa, she wanted to help find Nancy's killer.

"I noticed something on the sleeve of her coat. It was yellow." Cassie recalled the streak of yellow that stood out against the plum color of the coat that Nancy wore.

"I noticed it, too. I think it's a feather." Tessa glanced over at her. "I'm sure Ollie will bag it up."

"Could it have come off the wreath?" Cassie looked over at the massive ring of leaves, flowers, lights, and other assorted decorations. "I don't see any other feathers on it."

"It's possible, I guess. But I don't see any, either." Tessa glanced in the same direction. "I also noticed some scuff marks in the snow. But not enough for a full shoe print." She pulled out her phone. "I managed to take some pictures. It looks like there might be a partial pattern from a shoe." She held up her phone to show them to Cassie. "This isn't going to be an easy crime to solve. Just about the whole town is out on this farm today."

"Maybe the key will be the why?" Cassie

suggested. "Why would someone want Nancy dead? She seemed like a pretty nice person to me."

"She was a nice person." Tessa's voice softened. "She never did any harm to anyone, that I know about."

"What about her daughter?" Cassie met Tessa's eyes. "Maybe she held a grudge for the fact that her mother didn't keep her."

"Maybe. That's quite an extreme reaction, though. They should tell her soon. She shouldn't find out from gossip."

"Her sister is here, too. She was with her when she started off the scavenger hunt."

"Yes, her sister Sally. And her friend Marie. She had a lot of people who loved her."

"And one person who hated her enough to kill her," Cassie said.

"Maybe it wasn't meant to be a murder at all." Tessa swept her gaze around the area. "Maybe an argument spun out of control, and the ax happened to be nearby." She gestured to a fresh stump not far from the body. "It could have been left behind after some trees were felled."

"Or, by a criminal who was attempting to cut down trees illegally." Cassie's eyes widened. "Like Devon?"

"Like Devon. He's definitely a suspect, and he was here not long ago."

"I'm sure he's long gone by now."

"Probably." Tessa turned to face her. "We need to start by talking to as many people as we can. As of now, every person who had any kind of interaction with Nancy over the past few days, is a potential link to the truth about her murder." She glanced over at the officers. "Let's go see what we can find out."

Cassie followed Tessa toward the large crowd that had gathered near the parking lot. She noticed Sebastian beside an officer as they held back the onlookers. As much as she wanted to go talk to him, she focused her attention on the woman who Tessa walked toward.

Sally brushed her long, blonde hair back over her shoulders and took a deep breath. She stared at them as they approached.

Cassie hung back a few steps as Tessa crossed the small remaining distance between herself and Sally.

"Sally, have you spoken with Ollie?"

"No." Sally's stony expression didn't shift with her response. "But an officer told me what happened."

"I'm so sorry for your loss." Tessa looked into her eyes.

"Thank you." Sally crossed her arms. "I just want Nancy to still be here."

Tessa winced as Sally's stern expression crumbled into devastation.

"Oliver, what happened?" Sally stared over Tessa's shoulder at Oliver, who walked toward them. "Who did this?"

"We're still gathering information at this time. It's far too early to know who did this." Oliver stepped up beside them. The professional tone of his voice did nothing to soften his stern expression. "But I will do everything in my power to find the murderer."

"I just can't believe this happened. Nancy has always been the strong one. How can she be gone?" Sally covered her mouth as she began to weep.

"I'm so sorry, Sally." Tessa offered Sally a tissue.

"Sally, may I speak with you?" Oliver gestured to a small patio set close to the barn. "I just have a few questions for you."

Sally dabbed her eyes with the tissue she clutched.

"Of course, whatever I can do to help, I want to do." She followed him over to the table and chairs.

CHAPTER 4

"What's going on?" Nina's voice cracked as she rushed toward the group with Marie trailing a few steps behind her. "Why are there so many police here? What's happening?"

Cassie winced as she noticed that Oliver remained occupied with Sally. She glanced over at Tessa.

"Nina, I'm so sorry, but something terrible has happened." Tessa met Nina's eyes.

Marie stepped off a nearby path and walked toward them with a concerned expression.

"Nina, where's Nancy?"

"I don't know, but something has gone wrong." Nina looked in Sally's direction as Oliver leaned over the table to comfort her. "No, no, no! Don't tell me!" Nina gasped as she took a few steps back.

Marie scanned the crowd, which was a mixture of police officers and local residents, before looking back at Cassie and Tessa.

"It's Nancy, isn't it? I don't see her anywhere. I've been looking for her. I couldn't find her." Marie's voice trailed off as she looked back at Tessa. "It's not like her to go missing, especially during a big event. What's happened to her?"

"It can't be," Nina whimpered.

"I'm so sorry to tell you both this, but Nancy has been killed." Tessa locked her eyes to Nina's as a shriek burst past her lips.

"What?" Marie gulped. "Killed? I thought maybe there had been a terrible accident. Are you certain she's been killed?"

"Yes." Cassie watched as Tessa wrapped her arm around Nina to help her stay upright. "We're so sorry for your loss."

"Our loss?" Marie stared at the crowd. Her voice grew distant. "How did I lose her? I just saw her not long ago. I had to calm her down because she'd gotten so upset with Kevin. Then, when I went looking for her again, it was like she had vanished." Her eyes narrowed. "Was it Kevin who did this? He's the delivery driver. They were arguing over his job. Did he kill her because of it?"

"Unfortunately, at this time they don't know who did it, but the police are actively investigating to find out. The more that you can tell the detective about Nancy's most recent activities, the better the chance that the killer will be caught." Tessa looked toward Oliver. "He's speaking with Sally at the moment."

"What can we possibly know that would help? Nancy didn't do anything unusual, other than hosting this wonderful activity for the whole town. I guess this is the thanks she gets. If Ollie worked a little harder at keeping crime down around here instead of chasing after Mirabel, maybe this wouldn't have happened!" Marie scowled.

"Ollie is a great detective," Cassie said as Marie glared at her.

"What do you know? You haven't lived here long enough to have an opinion." Marie shook her head. "I don't think you can call this a safe town, if Nancy was just murdered on her very own farm."

"We have no idea what happened, yet." Tessa straightened her shoulders as she met Marie's eyes. "But I do know that this is quite a shock for you. I know how close you and Nancy were. Was there anything she was upset about? Or maybe worried about? Even the smallest thing could mean a lot to the investigation."

"I have nothing to say." Marie walked away.

Cassie bit into the tip of her tongue. Marie's behavior struck her as odd. Wouldn't she want to do everything she could to help catch her best friend's killer?

"I've only been here for a short time." Nina chewed on her bottom lip. "I have no idea what her life was really like. Now, I'll never know." Fresh tears filled her eyes. She turned and fled.

"This has to be a very confusing time for her. Or, she's really trying to put on a show for our benefit." Tessa watched as Nina blended in with the crowd still waiting to be questioned.

"Tessa! She just lost her mother."

"A mother she barely knew, and a mother she may have had a motive to kill." Tessa narrowed her eyes. "I can acknowledge that she has a reason to grieve, but that doesn't let her off the hook as a suspect."

"Marie didn't seem all that broken up about Nancy's death. At least, not the way I would expect her to be."

"Grief can cause some strange reactions. I've

seen people act like that before when faced with a loss." Tessa scanned the crowd. "Mark and Sebastian were helping set up water and snacks to keep people calm as they waited to give their statements. I thought they would have been back by now."

"There they are." Cassie waved to them. "We need to figure out who could have been with Nancy at the time of her murder. Unfortunately, I don't think there are any cameras around the farm, and even if there are, I doubt there are any that far out into the trees."

"And putting together a timeline of where people were at a certain time with a crowd like this, is going to be difficult. Luckily, we don't have a large span of time to account for. We know that Nancy was arguing with Kevin around the time the scavenger hunt started, and less than an hour later she was dead. We just have to find a way to fill in that time gap." Tessa walked toward the parking lot.

"We know something else." Cassie walked beside her. "Marie said she'd been looking for Nancy and wasn't able to find her. I'm not sure how much that helps."

"Actually, it does help. It tells us that maybe Nancy didn't want to be found. Why, after planning this big event, did she end up somewhere so far away from the crowd? Why wasn't she walking around interacting with the people on the scavenger hunt, or overseeing the refreshments in the parking lot?" Tessa snapped her fingers. "That's it. I know it. She had to be meeting with someone."

"I hadn't thought about that." Cassie's eyes widened. "Maybe someone didn't sneak up on her. Maybe she intended to meet her killer at that exact spot. Like you said, she probably didn't want to be seen. So, who would she be meeting with that she wouldn't want anyone else to know about?"

A smile crept across Tessa's lips as she nodded. "The father of her child. Who else?"

"That makes sense!" Cassie clicked her fingers together. "This whole time we've been focusing on Nina being Nancy's long-lost daughter, but she had a father, too. A father that might not want the truth getting out."

"Exactly. Nancy went to a lot of trouble to hide her pregnancy, but when Nina found her, she didn't turn her away. She invited her into her home. She made her part of this event. She wasn't afraid for the truth to come out. Maybe, Nancy was never the one who wanted to pretend Nina didn't exist. Maybe someone else pushed her to place the baby up for adoption and hide the pregnancy entirely." Tessa started toward her jeep. "We're not going to find out much more here. Let's go back to my place. I need to whip up some cookies for the Christmas parade, and we need to get to the bottom of who Nina's father is."

CHAPTER 5

Cassie followed Tessa toward her jeep. Maybe discovering who Nina's father was, would lead to important information about Nancy and her murder. But without a place to start, how would they ever figure it out?

Tessa tapped on Mark's shoulder as they walked past him in the parking lot. "Let's go."

Mark followed them to the jeep.

"I'll sit in the back." Cassie started to open the door of the jeep.

"Not a chance. No lady will sit in the back seat on my watch." Mark stepped past her and climbed into the back seat.

"Don't try to argue." Tessa glanced over her shoulder at Mark. "He's ridiculously stubborn."

"Huh, that never stops you from trying." Mark winked at Tessa.

"Well, I didn't say you were more stubborn than me." Tessa started the jeep.

"Is that even possible?" Cassie ducked as Tessa tried to swat at her arm.

"Eyes on the road, Tessa," Mark called out from the back seat.

"Eyes on your own business, Mark." Tessa whipped the jeep out onto the road.

Cassie thought about the events of the day as they drove toward Tessa's house. How had Nancy ended up dead?

"We would have won, you know?" Tessa parked in her driveway and got out of the jeep.

"I know that. We make a great team." Mark smiled as he stepped out of the jeep. "Keep in touch, Tessa. I know you'll be digging into all of this. If there's anything I can do to help, just let me know." He hugged her. Mark was one of the only people she let hug her. He pulled away and looked into her eyes. "Be careful, please."

"I will be." Tessa waved him off. "Go on now, we have things to do."

Tessa started through her gate as Mark headed toward his car.

She smiled as a collie mix bounded up to greet her. "Hi, Harry, it's good to see your sweet face." She crouched down and stroked the fur on his cheeks. "I missed you, too."

Harry licked her hands and gave a short bark.

"I know, I know. I should have taken you with me." Tessa straightened up. "Now, it's time to get to the truth."

As they stepped farther into Tessa's yard, two goats ran up to greet them.

Cassie reached into a bag in her pocket and fished out a handful of treats for the goats. She always made sure she had a bag of carrot pieces for them. She tossed the carrots to the goats and gave Harry a couple of dog treats.

"Sebastian is going to do some things on his farm, then he's going to meet us here later to go over some of the details." Cassie held her hand out to Harry to lick. "My mind is still trying to sort through all of this." She began pacing the length of the kitchen.

"Then let's help do just that. Let's see what we can find out about who Nancy really was. If she was capable of keeping a secret like Nina for so long, she might have been hiding other things as well." Tessa began mixing butter and sugar together.

"You're right. The more we know about her, the quicker we might discover why someone wanted her dead." Cassie sat down at the table and pulled her notebook out of her purse. She slid her phone a little closer. "I already started a list of suspects. I do think the fact that Kevin, the delivery driver, was seen arguing with Nancy shortly before she was killed, is a good lead. From what I overheard, the officers were looking for him, but people said he left the farm after the argument. I hope that Ollie can find him quickly, and maybe this will all get wrapped up right away."

"The argument is certainly an indication of motive, but I don't know." Tessa added some vanilla extract and an egg. "Why would he leave, and then come back to attack her?"

"Maybe he never left. Maybe he just made it look like he left, so that he could kill her and still have somewhat of an alibi." Cassie jotted a note down in her notebook. "Until we can confirm for sure that he actually left and was somewhere else when Nancy was killed, I still think he's a pretty good suspect."

"You're right." Tessa began mixing the ingredients together in the bowl. "But he's not the only suspect. Would he really be angry enough over a delivery job, to kill someone like that?"

"I guess it depends on how much damage the lost pay would do to him financially. If he was really counting on that money, maybe it could have inspired that much anger. But it would take some extreme circumstances. But he would likely also have an ax on his truck to trim down branches or cut down the base of the tree trunk, right?" Cassie made another note. "Which gives him both motive, and access to a weapon."

"All right, all right, fair point." Tessa began scooping flour into the bowl. "But I think we might need more information about Nancy before we can really know who might have been targeting her."

"On it now." Cassie began searching on her phone as she sat back in her chair. "I'm curious about who Nina's father was. Did he know about her? Did he pressure Nancy into hiding the pregnancy?"

"That's a good question. With Nina coming back into play, maybe it brought the father out of the woodwork. But it's also possible that the father had no idea about the baby."

"Very good point." Cassie jotted a few words in her notebook. "Although, if he did know, and he went to that much trouble to hide the fact that he had a child, it might be hard to figure out who he is." She paused as she skimmed over an article she'd found. "I found an article about the tree farm, written around about the time that Nancy would have been pregnant, if I'm doing my math right."

"Does it mention Nancy?" Tessa swapped over the dough in the fridge for some she had already prepared. She set the dough on a floured surface and began rolling it out.

"It does, but it says that she wasn't available for comment. It says that the farm was the first female-owned farm in the town, and that Nancy owned it and ran it with her sister Sally." Cassie looked up from her phone as Tessa began cutting out shapes from the dough. "That's pretty inspiring. It can't be easy work to tend to a tree farm."

"Nancy has always been a hard worker, from what I've known. Both Nancy and Sally kept to themselves. They were on the quiet side." Tessa placed several cookies onto a baking sheet as she continued. "Looking back, I guess that might be because they had something to hide."

"Do you think that Sally knew about the pregnancy?" Cassie tapped her pen against her notebook.

"I don't see how she could have missed it. Especially if they were running the farm together. Nancy had to give her a reason for disappearing for so long." Tessa slid the pan into the oven.

A few quick knocks drew Cassie's attention to the door. "Who could that be?"

"I doubt it's Ollie. He's probably still at the crime scene. Maybe Sebastian? Come on in!" Tessa called out.

Cassie stood up and walked toward the front door, eager to greet Sebastian. Before she could reach it, she heard a scurry of hooves and some muttered objections.

CHAPTER 6

The door swung open and Mirabel stepped inside. She pushed the door closed behind her with a swift shove and brushed a few pieces of grass from the snug jeans that covered her right hip. "Those goats are either too happy to see me, or really bad bodyguards."

"Probably a little of both." Tessa laughed.

"Am I late?" Cassie checked her watch. "I'm so sorry, I completely lost track of time. Who is at the diner?"

"Relax. Tamera is covering. I was going to spend some time with Maisy, but of course, all she wanted to do was go be with her friends. So, I thought I might come check on you two." Mirabel eyed the hot oven and the remnants of dough in the mixing bowl. "I figured I might find you like this." She looked at Cassie's notebook on the table. "Already hard at work solving the crime?"

"No offense to Ollie." Tessa wiped down the counter. "It never hurts to have a few extra eyes."

"I agree." Mirabel peeked at Cassie's phone. "Oh, you're not going to find much on the internet about Nancy. She's a very private person." She pulled a chair out from the table and sat down. "Luckily, you have me as a source of information. I know just about everything about her."

"Even that she had a child?" Tessa joined them at the table.

"No. At least, not exactly." Mirabel lowered her voice even though there was no one else in the room. "Nancy had an argument with her sister Sally, at the diner one night. I was just working as a waitress back then before my ex bought the place for me. I had no idea what the argument was about at the time, but now that I know about Nina, it all makes sense."

"Oh, what did they say?" Cassie leaned forward.

"Sally was trying to convince Nancy to tell everyone about something. I realize now it must have been about the pregnancy, and Nancy shut her down hard. She told her it wasn't her business, and she had already made the decision, and if she wanted to continue to have any contact with her, she should keep her mouth shut about it." Mirabel winced. "Given the way Nancy spoke to Sally, I thought Sally might fly across the table at her. But she didn't. She just went quiet. When I brought them their food, she wouldn't look at me, or Nancy, and her plate was still full when I cleared it." She sighed. "I always remembered that, because Sally and Nancy were normally quiet and easygoing."

"So, Sally knew about Nina?" Cassie scrolled through a few more results on her phone. "But she's also kept the secret all of these years, and we can assume that Marie knew about the baby, too, but also kept the secret. That seems almost impossible. What would cause them both to never slip up once over all this time?"

"Oh no, Marie didn't know. I'm sure of it." Mirabel shook her head.

"But they were good friends, weren't they?" Tessa asked.

"Yes, they were inseparable. But she didn't tell her." Mirabel put her mug back down on the table. "I'm not sure why Nancy never told her, but I do know that when Nina showed up claiming to be Nancy's daughter, and Nancy admitted to it, Marie was shocked. She nearly had a meltdown in the middle of the diner. I'd never seen her so flustered."

"Interesting." Cassie sat back in her chair and gazed up at the ceiling. "So Nancy fell pregnant, and obviously it wasn't planned. She knew she couldn't or didn't want to keep the baby, and she didn't want anyone to know about the child, either." She bit into her bottom lip. "I'm starting to think that Nina might have had a good motive to go after her mother. Maybe she ended up in a bad family situation?"

"Unfortunately, I don't know too much about Nina. I've tried to pry a little when I've seen her around town or in the diner, but she doesn't say more than two words at a time." Mirabel rolled her eyes.

"What about the father?" Tessa pulled a baking sheet out of the oven. She placed it on the stove to cool. "Do you know who the father was? Or have you heard any rumors about who he might be?"

"The father? That is a really good question. Unfortunately, no one seems to have any idea. We all suspect that he had to be someone from out of town, otherwise someone would have known about it. Right?" Mirabel looked between them. "Anyway, I do have a tip for you two. From what I heard,

Ollie can't find Kevin. I think I know where he might be, but you have to promise not to tell Ollie who told you."

"A tip that you'd rather give us than Ollie?" Tessa met her eyes. "Why is that?"

"Because, although Ollie isn't too fond of this, I have all kinds of friends, and some of them deal in not so legal situations. I don't want a friend to lose their business because Ollie finds out about it. Understand?" Mirabel glanced between the two of them. "I figured that you two might be a bit more discreet."

"We absolutely can be." Tessa turned off the oven. "Just tell us where to go."

"I'll give you the address." Mirabel met Tessa's eyes as her voice hardened. "But don't leave Cassie alone in there, and don't tell anyone that I'm the one that tipped you off. Deal?"

"I never reveal my sources." Tessa glanced over at Cassie. "And I won't take my eyes off her."

"Good." Mirabel patted Cassie's cheek as she smiled. "She's my best employee, and a great friend, I can't let anything happen to her."

"I'll be fine, I promise." Cassie grinned.

"What is the place, anyway?" Tessa grabbed her keys from a hook on the kitchen wall.

"It's a private social club. It has a bar and everything. They like to be discreet. Fly under the radar." Mirabel tapped her fingertips against the table.

"Do you think he would be there now? It's still quite early." Tessa looked at her.

"If he's stressed, possibly," Mirabel said. "He likes to drink."

"It's worth a try." Tessa glanced at Cassie.

"How bad could this place be, anyway?" Cassie asked.

"It depends on the day." Mirabel winced.

"That sounds like a story I want to hear." Cassie stepped closer to her. "Was your ex-husband involved with them?"

Mirabel's husband used to own the diner, and he had been involved with some shady people.

"Never mind. We're not talking about me right now." Mirabel smiled as she waved Cassie away. "Direct that curiosity where it can do some good. The past is the past." She handed Tessa a slip of paper, then turned toward the door. "I'll text you what else you'll need to know in order to get inside. It can be a little complicated." She peeked through the window on the door. "Would you mind calling off your monsters before I go out there?"

"Just let Harry out first. He'll keep them busy." Tessa clapped her hands at the collie mix curled up on his bed near the front door.

Harry jumped to his feet.

"Great." Mirabel gripped the knob, then turned it slowly.

Harry burst past her and began barking at the goats.

The goats scurried off around the side of the house as Harry chased after them.

Mirabel hurried toward her car.

"We'd better get to the jeep while we have the chance." Tessa stepped out onto the porch. "Harry can only keep them at bay for so long."

CHAPTER 7

Cassie followed after Tessa. As she settled in the passenger side of Tessa's jeep, her heart raced. She didn't know what to expect at the private club, but she did know that Nancy's murderer could potentially be there.

"Don't you think we should tell Ollie about this?"

"No. We'll handle it. I'll be at your side." Tessa started the jeep, then pulled out of the driveway. "Don't worry, I have acquaintances that wear badges, and ones on the wrong side of the law, too." She headed to the neighboring town of Rombsby.

"Why doesn't that make me feel better?" Cassie leaned back in her seat and texted Sebastian to let him know they wouldn't be at the house.

Tessa's cell phone began to ring inside her purse.

"Do you want me to grab that for you?" Cassie reached for Tessa's purse.

"Don't bother, it's just Mark." Tessa turned onto a side street.

"Are you psychic now?" Cassie grinned.

"I can tell by the ringtone." Tessa slowed the jeep down and began to crawl past the large houses that lined the street.

"He has his own ringtone now?" Cassie raised her eyebrows. "That's interesting."

"It's just easier to know who's calling." Tessa slowed down even more. "It should be right here."

"Do you think this is the place?" Cassie peered out through the window at the unremarkable home Tessa parked beside. "It just looks like someone's house."

"It's the address Mirabel gave me." Tessa pointed to a clump of trees near the driveway. "And that looks like a pretty big parking lot that those trees are hiding. Who needs that much parking for a regular house?"

"There are a few cars parked." Cassie surveyed the house again. "I guess there must be people inside."

"Let's find out." Tessa walked up to the front

door. She consulted the note that Mirabel had written for her, then knocked on the door three times. She stepped off to the side and rapped on the window beside the door twice.

A moment later, the front door swung open. A short, thin man leaned out and looked them over.

"Are you sure you two belong here?"

"I'm sure." Tessa's voice hardened as she gave him the password Mirabel had written down. "Red herring." She tried to hide her smile at the silliness of it all. "Are you going to let us in or not?"

"Fine, fine." He stepped back and gestured for them to move past him.

The dim lighting inside the house made the strange furnishings difficult to identify.

"What is this place?" Cassie whispered under her breath as she stayed close to Tessa's side. "I can barely see anything."

"Downstairs." The man near the door pointed to a single glowing purple light that hovered over a half-hidden staircase.

"It doesn't even look like a house," Cassie murmured as she followed Tessa down the stairs.

"Because it's not." Tessa descended the last step. "Like Mirabel said, it's some sort of private social club."

Music pounded through speakers mounted on the walls. A long bar stretched from one side of the room to the other. A few people occupied barstools lined up in front of it.

"I don't get it." Cassie frowned. "Why do they need to have a private club?"

"It's about being off the grid. A place you can go that not too many people know about or have access to. They're often open all hours, even when bars legally have to be closed." Tessa glanced over at her. "Sometimes they're up to criminal activity as well."

"I'm surprised there are quite a few people drinking at this time. It's still early." Cassie glanced at her watch. "It's not even three, yet."

"I wonder if Kevin is here." Tessa walked closer to the bar to get a better view. "I thought, maybe after the events of the day, he would want to blow off some steam."

"Tessa, there he is." Cassie pointed to a man slumped over the bar. "I'm pretty sure that's Kevin."

"Yes, that would be him." Tessa's tone softened as she stepped closer to Cassie. "And from the looks of it, he's had a few too many, already. Let me take the lead on this one. Stay back unless I call you forward."

"Tessa, you don't have to protect me." Cassie

met her eyes. "I don't want you to be in danger, either."

"Drunk people can be unpredictable, Cassie. Trust me. Just let me take the lead." Tessa moved in a casual stride toward the bar.

Cassie waited a few seconds before following after Tessa. She noticed the tension that rippled through Tessa's shoulders beneath her button-down blouse. She kept her muscles rigid as she paused beside Kevin.

"Kevin Burkson?"

Kevin shot up on the barstool so fast that he nearly toppled over the back of it.

Tessa grabbed his arm and kept him steady as he wobbled on the stool.

"Who wants to know?" Kevin's slurred speech indicated Tessa's assessment had been correct.

"I do." Tessa peered into his eyes. "Kevin, I'm here to talk to you about Nancy."

"No, no, no!" Kevin whimpered and slouched forward against the top of the bar again. "Please don't arrest me. I didn't do it. I promise. I really didn't."

"Kevin, I'm not here to arrest you." Tessa maintained her hand's position on his shoulder. "I'm here to ask you about what happened. You were likely one of the last people who saw Nancy alive. We're trying to find out the truth."

"Don't you mean, you're trying to accuse me of murder?" Kevin tilted his head to the side and looked up at her. "I'm already guilty, aren't I? That's what everyone is going to think. I knew it would only be a matter of time before someone showed up to arrest me. I don't think there's anything I can say to prove my innocence."

"You could start with where you were earlier." Tessa held his gaze. "After you argued with Nancy, where did you go?"

"I left. I went for a drive." Kevin winced. "Great alibi, right?"

"It could be. Did anyone see you go for this drive? Did you stop anywhere for gas? Snacks?" Tessa leaned closer to him. "You have to give me something here, Kevin."

"I have nothing to give." Kevin sat up. "I just drove around. Then I went back to my apartment, and I saw what happened, on the news. I knew I'd be the main suspect, so I came here to wait it out."

"All right, then let's start at the beginning. Why were you arguing with Nancy in the first place? The whole day was supposed to be about celebrating the holiday. What did you have to be upset about?" Tessa leaned against the side of the bar.

Cassie noticed the way her muscles remained coiled, ready to spring. She guessed that Tessa still saw Kevin as a threat, even with his intoxication.

"The holiday?" A forced laugh burst past Kevin's lips. "What holiday? You know, when my wife left me, I thought I was doing the right thing by letting her have full custody. I thought a mother should be with her children, and I'll still be part of their lives. Now, I'm just the guy that shows up with gifts. That's it. They do everything else with her. But this year, I can't even be that. Because Nancy refused to pay me because a delivery was stolen. She said it was my fault because I went into a shop for just a few minutes to buy a coffee."

"Oh, that was bad luck," Tessa said.

"It was. Nancy said I never should have left the trees alone on the truck. But I'd been working extra shifts to earn more money for Christmas, and I was tired. I didn't feel safe driving, so I just wanted to grab a quick coffee. When I came back out, the truck was gone." Kevin squeezed his eyes shut and shook his head. "I know I shouldn't have left the trees, but it was just for a few minutes. Without that money, I have nothing to buy gifts for my kids!"

"You must have been desperate," Tessa said.

"I was." Kevin slumped down against the bar again. "She owed me for a few deliveries. I begged her to pay me. I asked her to just pay me, and she could take money out of my next few paychecks to compensate for the trees. But she refused. She said that I needed to learn from my mistakes, and if hurting my wallet was the only way I would learn, then that was what she would do." He glared at Tessa. "Can you believe that? How could she be so cruel? I bet she never had to struggle for a single thing in her life."

"I can see why you would be so angry at her." Tessa frowned. "All you needed was a break, and she wouldn't give you that."

"Exactly. So, yes, I yelled. But I didn't kill her." Kevin sat up, then stood up. He swayed as he looked straight at Tessa. "I wouldn't do that!"

"Easy now, Kevin." Tessa grabbed his elbow before he could stumble over another barstool. "I think you've had enough. It's time to get you home."

"No." Kevin pulled away from her and swayed again. "I don't even have a home to go to. An empty apartment? Bills piled up? An empty refrigerator? No. I'm not going anywhere."

"You're wrong about that." Oliver's stern tone coincided with the abrupt silencing of the music that had pounded through the speakers mounted on the walls.

CHAPTER 8

The few people who occupied the bar area fled toward the stairs, while the bartender ducked down behind the bar.

The man who had let them in hovered near the doorway and clasped his hands together in front of him.

"It's all right, folks. He promised no trouble."

The bartender peeked over the edge of the bar.

"I'm not here to cause any problems." Oliver met the bartender's eyes. "I just need to speak with him." He shifted his gaze to Kevin.

Kevin sank back down on the barstool. "Of course you're here for me."

Oliver's eyes skipped from Tessa, to Cassie, then back to Tessa again. "Who tipped you off?"

"The important thing is that Kevin here doesn't have an alibi." Tessa cleared her throat.

"I didn't do it!" Kevin snapped. "Listen, listen! I wasn't going to say anything, but I think I know who did kill Nancy."

"You think you know, or you know?" Oliver asked. "Did you see it happen? Were you there?"

"No, I wasn't there when she was killed. But I was there when someone threatened to kill her." Kevin's voice began to even out as he sat more upright. "I heard the two of them fighting, and when Nancy wouldn't do what she wanted her to do, she threatened to kill her."

"Who threatened her?" Oliver leaned closer to him. "Who did you hear?"

"It was Nina, her daughter." Kevin wobbled on the barstool. "I went there to plead with Nancy for my pay, but when I got there, she and Nina were arguing. It got really loud. They started screaming at each other. Nancy said something like, it's my responsibility and I have to do it, and Nina shouted at her that she would kill her." He held up his hands and swayed backward. "Look, I don't know if she really did it, I just know that she threatened to."

"It's pretty easy to point the finger at someone else." Oliver grabbed him under his arm and pulled him to his feet. "When you know that you're the best suspect."

"I didn't do it." Kevin squirmed in his grasp.

"What about the theft of the trees? Did you do that?" Oliver stared hard into his eyes.

"What?" Kevin wobbled from side to side. "What are you talking about? Of course I didn't steal the trees. I lost so much money because of it."

"Or maybe you saw a chance to make a lot more money? I've seen your financials. I've also spoken to your ex-wife. She told me that you're supposed to be covering the gifts for Christmas and that you'd be here wasting what little money you did have. So, I know you needed the cash, Kevin. When someone came to you with a plan to steal the trees and resell them for pure profit, I bet you jumped at the chance."

"No, I didn't! I don't know what you're talking about! Someone stole my truck!"

"Which you just happened to leave alone just long enough for the thief to steal. You left the keys in the truck, Kevin. Who does that?" Oliver guided him to lean back against the bar. "I want some answers."

"I don't have any!" Kevin moaned. "I just went

in to grab a coffee and came right back out. When I did, the truck was gone. That's all I know!"

"And a few hours later, we found your truck in the field, only the trees were missing. Lucky you, huh?" Oliver glared at him.

"Lucky me? No!" Kevin pointed at himself. "I lost my pay for some deliveries! Do you know how much money I'll lose because of that? It's the busiest time of year."

"What I know is that you don't have an alibi. You were seen arguing with Nancy, and there's a good chance that you were in on the theft of her trees. Is that why she refused to pay you? Because she knew that you were part of the plan?" Oliver asked.

"I didn't know about the theft! I didn't kill Nancy! I had nothing to do with any of it! Please, just let me go!" Kevin pleaded.

"I'm afraid I can't do that." Oliver held out a set of handcuffs. "You're going to need to come down to the station with me."

"Fine." Kevin held out his hands. "Go ahead. Arrest me. My life can't get much worse."

"It might. Where's your ax?" Oliver closed the handcuffs around his wrists. "The one that's usually on your truck?"

"It should be on there." Kevin shrugged. "I haven't moved it."

"It's not. I looked before I came in here." Oliver shot a quick look at Tessa, then focused on Kevin again. "Maybe you left it behind with Nancy, after you killed her?"

"No! There's no way! It probably got stolen with the trees. I haven't used it since then."

"You never reported it missing." Oliver steered him toward the door. "Why wouldn't you look for it?"

"I didn't even think about it." Kevin stumbled forward.

"We'll look after you at the station. Get you sobered up, so you can answer some questions." Oliver led Kevin toward the door. He looked at the doorman as he walked past him. "I'm going to have to make sure the local police know about this place."

Cassie nudged Tessa's arm with her elbow. "Ollie didn't look too happy."

"He's just annoyed that we got here first." Tessa slipped a business card to the doorman as she stepped past him. "Give this man a call. He might be able to help you out if the police come back."

"Thanks." The doorman put the card in his pocket.

"Why did you help him?" Cassie followed Tessa up the stairs. "If there are illegal things happening here, do you really think they should be allowed to stay in business?"

"It's not my place to decide that. I just know that everyone's entitled to a defense and Mark might be able to help him out."

"I guess you're right about that. Do you believe Kevin? Do you really think he didn't do it?" Cassie stepped out of the house behind Tessa.

"I think we need to find out what Nina and Nancy were arguing about this morning. From what I overheard, she didn't mention a word about it during her interview. That makes me think she's hiding something." Tessa opened the driver's side door to the jeep. "What do you say we take a drive back out to the farm?"

"Sounds good to me." Cassie climbed into the passenger side. "But if she wouldn't talk about it in her interview, what makes you think you can get her to talk about it now?"

"I'm not going to try to get her to talk. I'm going to take a look around the farm, while you try to talk to her and distract her. The murderer had to change somewhere, and might have stashed their clothes nearby," Tessa said.

"That's true."

"There wasn't much time between the murder and when the body was found. There are many places on the property the murderer could have accessed water to clean up. If they needed to hide their clothes fast, they might have thought the storage shed would be a good place to leave them until they could get back to them. It's the closest building to the wreath, and I think it's the best place to start. It had snowed early this morning, just before the scavenger hunt started. It was chilly enough for everyone to be wearing coats. Maybe the killer took their coat off, killed Nancy, and then put their coat back on. Maybe they hid their clothes that way or managed to take them off the farm with them another way. But there's a chance they're still there." Tessa glanced at Cassie as she started the jeep. "You just have to keep her talking. But be very careful not to tip her off that we suspect her. If she gets nervous, she might shut us down before I have the chance to look around."

"Don't worry, I'll keep her busy." Cassie peered at the road ahead of them.

CHAPTER 9

Cassie watched a parade of police cars roll past them as Tessa parked the jeep just outside the entrance of the farm.

"My guess is they haven't released the crime scene, yet, but they are done with their search." Tessa stepped out of the jeep.

"Don't you think the police would have searched the storage shed?" Cassie stepped out as well.

"Yes. But with a property as vast as this, with so many outbuildings, and such a large farmhouse, I think there's a good chance they overlooked something. It doesn't hurt to check again." Tessa pulled her phone out of her purse. "I'm going to call you. Leave the line open so that I can hear you. If you can't keep Nina away from the shed, say it looks like snow, and I'll know to bolt. Got it?"

"It looks like snow." Cassie pulled out her phone and answered Tessa's call. She slipped her phone into her back pocket. "Just be careful, Tessa."

"You, too. Once you have her distracted, say I'm so sorry, and I'll know it's safe for me to slip into the storage shed. Okay?"

"Yes, got it." Cassie walked off toward the main barn. As she approached it, she noticed Nina standing not far from the barn. A man clung to the top of a ladder as he reached for some Christmas lights.

"Just take them down, please." Nina clasped her hands together in front of her as the worker disconnected the string of lights from the edge of the barn. "I don't want to see any of these decorations anymore."

"Nina?" Cassie stepped up beside her as the lights fell to the ground beside the ladder. "How are you doing?"

"I just need to stay busy." Nina turned to look at Cassie. "It's the only thing that keeps me from focusing on it. The decorations make me too upset. They just remind me that I didn't get to spend a

Christmas with her. I think the sooner all this festive stuff is down, the sooner I'll be able to move on."

"I'm so sorry you're going through this. Do you have any other family close by that can help you with all of this? Maybe your aunt, Sally?" Cassie swept her gaze over the handful of workers that continued to remove the decorations.

"My aunt?" Nina snapped the words. "I don't want anything to do with her!"

"You don't?" Cassie's eyes widened. "But she's your family."

"Not at all! She refused to accept me. My mother tried to convince her that she should welcome me, but Sally insisted I was just a stranger." Nina shook her head. "When I first came here, I thought Nancy might reject me. But she didn't. She welcomed me home. But Sally? She kept telling Nancy that I had no business here and that she needed to tell me to leave. I didn't know why then, but I do now."

"Why?" Cassie searched her eyes. "Why did Sally have such a problem with you?"

"I've heard from my mother's estate lawyer. He said that when I came here, my mother changed her will, and that she left me the farm and the majority of her wealth. My guess is that Sally found out about that and was quite angry about it." Nina crossed her arms. "I thought she might be willing to talk to me, share our grief over my mother's death, so I went to her. She refused to open the door to her house, and she won't answer her phone. I hate to think this, because it would be horrible to imagine my mother dying at the hands of her sister, but as cold and cruel as she is, I'm starting to think it's possible that Sally is the one who killed her."

"Have you ever seen her be violent?" Cassie raised her eyebrows.

"No, but I haven't known her for very long. She was so determined to make sure that I knew how important she was to my mother, she would show up whenever I was around, and try to drive us apart. I guess I didn't really have much of a chance to get to know Sally because I was too busy defending myself to her. I kept telling her that I was only here to get to know Nancy, not to cause her any stress, but she kept insisting that I didn't belong here." Nina wiped a tear from her cheek. "I don't even know what to think. It's amazing that she left me all of this, but I would much rather have her here with me."

"I'm sure you would." Cassie smiled slightly. "I hope that you know how much she must have loved you to leave you with such a gift."

"I guess." Nina sighed. "It doesn't explain why she left me behind when I was born, or why she wouldn't tell me about my father."

"She never even gave you a hint?" Cassie asked.

"No. If I brought it up, she would get very angry. She told me that I needed to leave the past in the past and focus on our future together. But I didn't think that was very fair. Maybe her relationship with my father was in the past, but he's still my father now. Right?"

"Right." Cassie nodded. "Do you have any suspicions about who he might be? Did you do any of your own research?"

"I tried, but I couldn't get anywhere. I figured that my mother would tell me eventually. But now she'll never have the chance. Sally might know, but she'll never tell me." Nina closed her eyes. "I just want this whole day to have been a bad dream."

"I understand that." Cassie met her eyes as she opened them. "My guess is that you were probably the closest person to Nancy in her final days. Did you notice anything off about her? Did she mention being afraid of anyone?"

"Afraid? No." Nina smiled some. "I'm not sure that she knew the meaning of that word. She was quiet, but she had a very strong personality. She'd been hunting down Devon, the guy that's been stealing trees. She was determined to catch him in the act and make sure that he was stopped."

"She was pretty serious about stopping him from stealing the trees, huh? She was pretty hard on Kevin about the stolen trees, too." Cassie narrowed her eyes. "Did you know about that?"

"It wasn't just about stealing the trees. When you take a tree from the ground, it affects the entire environment around it. Taking the wrong tree at the wrong time can be devastating for an entire ecosystem. She was passionate about life, especially nature itself. As for Kevin, she was furious that he'd left his truck with the trees piled on it. Not just because they were stolen, but because he had assured her that he would deliver them straight to the customers. She took her business and her reputation very seriously, and to have him not deliver when he was supposed to was a hit to her reputation and her income."

"That makes sense. Do you think that she ever found any evidence that could be used against Devon?"

"I know she had these." Nina pulled her phone out of her pocket, tapped the screen a few times, then held it up for Cassie to see. "That's Devon entering protected land two nights ago. Unfortunately, she wasn't able to catch him bringing anything back out. But she had been following him whenever she could."

"If Devon thought she might have had more evidence, that might have been a motive for him to kill her." Cassie looked at the pictures.

"I sent the pictures to the detective. I'm not sure if they'll help." Nina slid her phone back into her pocket. "I wouldn't doubt that Devon had something to do with it."

"Thanks for the information, Nina. If I find out anything, I'll let you know. Okay?" Cassie looked into her eyes.

"Sure, I guess. I'm not sure that it will matter. It won't change the fact that she's gone." Nina squinted at a group of workers gathered near a large, decorated Christmas tree. "Why are you just standing there? Take it all down!" She spun around toward another worker. "No! Not in the barn! Put it all in the shed. I'm going to make sure everything gets donated."

Cassie's heart skipped a beat as she realized Tessa might still be inside the shed.

"It looks like snow, doesn't it?" She squinted up at the clear blue sky.

"What?" Nina looked up as well. "There isn't a cloud in sight."

"I guess I'm just hoping. After getting a taste of it this morning." Cassie offered an awkward smile. "It's always nice to have a white Christmas."

"No amount of snow is going to make this a good Christmas." Nina turned and walked off toward the shed.

Cassie held her breath.

"All clear," Tessa's voice called out from her back pocket.

CHAPTER 10

"I was so worried you were still in the shed." Cassie hurried through the main entrance of the farm and met Tessa at her jeep. "Did you find anything?"

"No, unfortunately not. I searched through the entire storage shed, and all I found were tools and supplies." Tessa climbed into the driver's seat. "What about you? Did Nina give you any new details? I couldn't hear everything that she said."

"A few. Nancy refused to tell her about her father. Sally absolutely did not like her, and apparently Nancy left just about everything to Nina." Cassie buckled her seat belt. "Which explains why Sally is not too fond of her."

"Oh, wow." Tessa started the jeep. "Do you

think that Sally found out and killed her sister out of anger?"

"Maybe. Or maybe she didn't know if the will had been changed, yet, and she hoped that killing her would prevent her from being able to officially change it." Cassie's phone rang in her purse. She dug it out as she continued. "But she seems more convinced that Devon, the guy who is apparently stealing trees that Ollie argued with earlier today, is the one who was after her. Hold on, it's Sebastian." She put the phone to her ear. "Hi, where are you?" She paused as her eyes widened. "Hang on, I'm going to put you on speaker, so you can give Tessa the address." She set the phone in the middle console.

"We're at Seventeen Creekside. There's a big RV out front. Stephanie's certain that she just saw Devon go into it."

"Devon?" Tessa turned down a side street. "How did she manage to find him?"

"We were just driving past and we spotted him." Sebastian drew a breath. "I didn't see him myself, but Stephanie is sure she saw him."

"I did see him." Stephanie's voice carried through the phone.

"Stephanie called Ollie, but he's not picking up,"

Sebastian said.

"When we saw him last, he was taking Kevin in for questioning. He's probably busy with him," Tessa said.

"Sebastian, look! He's coming back out and heading for that car. If he gets away, we might not be able to find him again!" Stephanie's voice raised slightly with a sense of urgency.

"I have to go, Cassie." Sebastian ended the call.

"Sebastian!" Cassie stared at the phone. "Tessa, hurry up. We don't want Devon to get away."

"I'm already stepping on the gas." Tessa leaned forward in her seat. "Devon is not the kind of person to surprise. He has a history of criminal behavior."

"He's not picking up, neither is Stephanie!" Cassie groaned as she ended the call. "Are we close?"

"It's just around the corner here." Tessa whipped around the corner of Creekside and slowed down at the sight of a large RV.

Sebastian and Stephanie were standing in front of Devon outside it. It looked like they were blocking his path.

"Sebastian, Stephanie." Cassie jumped out of the jeep and ran toward them.

"I need to get out of here." Devon started to step past Sebastian.

"We just want to ask you some questions." Tessa stepped in front of him. "What's the harm in that?"

"What questions?" Devon looked over at her. "I didn't do anything wrong!"

"I wonder if Nancy would agree with that?" Cassie took a step toward him. "Were you so scared that she had evidence against you that you decided she had to die?"

"I didn't kill her!" Devon leaned against the RV. "I know that's what everyone is going to think. I know that with my history, it'll be easy to assume that I'm just a criminal. But I wouldn't kill anyone. I didn't kill Nancy, even though I had every right to go after her."

"Go after her?" Stephanie pursed her lips. "What's that supposed to mean?"

"She was the one stalking me! I was about to file charges against her for harassment! She had no proof I was doing anything wrong! She wouldn't leave me alone!" Devon scowled.

"That had to make you pretty angry." Tessa shook her head. "Angry enough to make sure she couldn't bother you anymore?"

"No." Devon took a step toward them. "No, I

didn't do that. I was only there today because I thought I should tell her the truth about her daughter."

"What truth?" Tessa's stern tone made him stop walking. "Tell me now, Devon, because the moment that Ollie gets here, he's going to make sure you talk, and I won't be able to do anything to stop him and help you."

"She's a scam artist." Devon looked straight into Tessa's eyes. "She's not Nancy's kid. She's just someone pretending to be her! As much of a pain as Nancy was to me, I couldn't just stand back and watch her get taken like that. I mean, she really believed that Nina was her kid. She didn't bother with a DNA test, she just believed her."

"So, you told her that?" Cassie spoke up. "You went to Nancy and told her that Nina was a scam artist, and I bet Nancy knew you were lying to her. She probably accused you of just trying to ruin her life. You two argued, and that's when you snapped. Right?"

"Wrong." Devon sighed. "Look, I went there to tell her. I thought it was the right thing to do. But I never had the chance to. That detective ran me off before I could say a word to her. That's when I realized it didn't matter, anyway."

"It didn't matter that Nina was pretending to be Nancy's daughter, or that Nancy would never believe your lies?" Stephanie asked.

"It didn't matter because I knew that she wouldn't listen. I knew the detective wouldn't listen. To them, I'm just a criminal. That's all I'll ever be. I wanted to do a good thing, but it wouldn't have mattered." Devon groaned as a patrol car pulled up beside the RV. "I didn't do it. Someone has to believe me."

"You're going to have to explain that to the police." Tessa watched as Oliver stepped out of the car.

"I'll take it from here." Oliver walked toward Devon. "It's time for all of you to leave."

Cassie thought that Tessa might protest. But instead, she just turned and walked toward her jeep. As Cassie followed Tessa, she listened to Oliver's conversation. He wasn't going to arrest Devon but was taking him in for questioning.

Cassie, Tessa, Sebastian, and Stephanie stood by Tessa's jeep.

"Why did you give in so easily?" Cassie watched as Oliver's car pulled away with Devon in the back.

"Because, we've done all we can for today." Tessa opened her jeep door. "I think my brain needs a break. I need to process all of this. In the morning, though, I want to go speak with Sally. If what Devon said is true, then Sally might have known about it, too. I want to see what she thinks about it all." Tessa smiled as she looked between Sebastian and Stephanie. "You handled Devon very nicely."

"We just wanted to make sure he didn't run. If he did, he might have disappeared." Stephanie put her hands on her hips. "I hope Ollie can get the truth out of him."

"I'm sure he will." Tessa waved to them as she climbed into her jeep.

CHAPTER 11

Tessa wanted to talk things through with Mark. She always found it helpful to go over things with him, especially when she was investigating something. After hearing what Devon had to say, she needed some legal information, and Mark was her best source for that. It was getting late, and she thought about waiting until the morning to see him, but he was a night owl, and she doubted he would be up early the following morning. She was eager to find out the information as quickly as possible.

She drove past his house, but there were no lights on inside. So, she decided to try his office. As she turned into the parking lot, she noticed his car in its usual parking space.

She parked, grabbed the bag of cookies she'd brought with her for situations like this, then stepped out of her jeep. She walked up the stairs to his outer office door. The lights were on, and the door opened when she turned the knob. But there was no one at the receptionist desk, which was no surprise given the time.

Tessa walked over to his inner office and gave a light knock on the open door.

"Mark." Tessa smiled as he looked up at her.

"Sorry, I didn't see you there." Mark stood up and walked around his desk. He opened his arms and hugged her.

"You're working late?"

"I had a few things I needed to get done, and after the events of today, I doubted I would be able to sleep."

"Can I pick your brain?" Tessa held up the plastic bag. "I brought cookies."

"You don't have to bring me cookies. You're welcome here any time." Mark stepped back from her.

"Oh, okay then, I'll just stick these back in the jeep." Tessa smiled.

"Don't you dare." Mark snatched the bag from her hand as he laughed.

"I thought you might like them." Tessa stepped past him into the office.

"Thank you." Mark walked around his desk. "Let me guess, this is about Nancy."

"Yes." Tessa pulled her phone out of her purse. "Or more specifically, Nina." She pulled up a picture of her on her phone. "When we spoke with Devon just before, he said something strange that's made me want to know more about her."

"You spoke with him?" Mark smiled. "He's a dangerous character. Is he okay?"

"What?"

"I've seen you 'speak with' people before. I'm just wondering if you sent him running."

"Ha, very funny." Tessa gave a short laugh. "No, I didn't really get the chance to talk to him much. Sebastian and Stephanie made sure he didn't get away, and Ollie arrived shortly after Cassie and me."

"Sebastian? The farmer?" Mark chuckled. "That I find hard to believe."

"Apparently, he has a little more spunk to him than any of us realized. Anyway, Devon said something about Nina not actually being Nancy's daughter. It got me thinking, what do we really know about Nina? I realized I don't know very much about the adoption process, either." Tessa set her phone down on his desk. "And we also found out today that Nina expects to inherit just about all of her mother's estate, because Nancy had recently changed her will. Do you think that's legal, yet? Or will Sally be able to contest it because Nina was not actually raised by Nancy?"

"So, you're hoping for a little legal expertise?" Mark opened the bag of cookies. "Good thing you brought a bribe." He took a bite of a cookie, then sat back against his seat. "To start with, the adoption process can either be legal and well documented, or illegal and almost impossible to track down."

"Nina found her mother, though, so she had to have been able to get information from somewhere, right? Mirabel says that Nancy was determined to hide the pregnancy and the baby. My guess is she would have insisted that all information be kept very private."

"That may be true, but laws have changed over the years, giving children who are adopted more rights to finding out about their parentage. A lot depends on the state she was actually born in. Nancy didn't have the baby here, which means she might have had Nina in another state entirely. But I can tell you that if Nancy just left everything to

Nina in her will, the lawyer in charge of the estate will want to verify that Nina is actually who she says she is. He'll need to prove her identity." Mark took another bite of the cookie, then moaned. "This is really good. You have a magic touch in the kitchen, Tessa."

"I'm glad you like it. You can help me frost some, so they're ready for the parade." Tessa picked up her phone again. "So, if Nina isn't who she says she is, then she might not be able to inherit the estate?"

"It's not so much about her being Nancy's actual daughter. It's more about her legal name. Nancy left the money to Nina specifically, so only Nina can claim it. Do you really think that the person we met this morning isn't Nancy's daughter?" Mark raised an eyebrow. "That would be quite surprising."

"I'm not sure. She obviously claims to be, and she hasn't given any indication that she's being deceitful. But how would Nancy even know? If she hadn't seen Nina since the day she was born, she certainly wouldn't be able to recognize her. I wonder if she even looked into her and verified her identity?" Tessa sat back against the chair. "Then again, maybe I'm grasping at straws."

"Your instincts are always sharp." Mark tilted

his head to the side. "I have no doubt that if you sense something is off, it is."

"Maybe, but sensing it isn't enough." Tessa stood up from the chair. "Thanks for your help, Mark."

"Why don't you stay for a while." Mark stood up. "You don't have to go."

"I need to do some research." Tessa started toward the door. "I'll catch up with you tomorrow."

"Great." Mark walked with her to the door. "I'm always here for you."

"Thanks, Mark." Tessa slipped out through the door and hurried down the stairs toward her jeep.

CHAPTER 12

When Cassie awoke the following morning, the events of the previous day came flooding back, and she quickly remembered she had plans with Tessa to try and help figure out who killed Nancy. She got up and had a shower.

As she came out of the shower, the aroma of fresh coffee and the sound of sizzling bacon greeted her. Sebastian!

She quickly got ready and headed downstairs. As she walked past the living room, she smiled as she remembered the Christmas decorations she and Sebastian had already put up. The lights were strung in the windows, and they had put an inflatable snowman and Santa in the front yard, along with an assortment of lights. At the time she thought it might have been too much, but the local children loved walking past. Now she just needed a Christmas tree.

"Morning."

"Morning." Sebastian's smile spread as she walked across the kitchen to hug him.

"This is a nice surprise."

"I wanted to make you breakfast." Sebastian walked over to the stove. "I have a busy day, but I wanted to spend some time with you."

"I am so happy to see you."

"You have time for breakfast, right?" Sebastian grabbed the spatula and slid some slices of bacon and eggs onto a plate for her.

"Absolutely." Cassie took the plate and kissed his cheek. "Thanks so much, Sebastian. You didn't have to do all of this."

"I did it because I wanted to." Sebastian poured coffee into two mugs. "You spend all day serving others at the diner, the least I can do is take care of you when I get a chance."

"You're too amazing." Cassie sat down at the kitchen table and picked up a piece of bacon. "I love working at the diner, but I've never been much into cooking. I don't think about cooking too much when

I'm at home." She scrunched up her nose. "But you never complain about that, when I should be making you meals."

"Why?" Sebastian set a mug of coffee down in front of her. "I have nothing to complain about, Cassie. I always love spending time with you."

"I don't know, I guess because that's more traditional. The woman cooks for the man." Cassie took another bite of her bacon. "I always cooked for my husband before. Not that it was any good or he appreciated it, but a lot of the time we'd have things catered or go out to eat."

"I can't compare to fancy chefs." Sebastian grinned as he sat down across from her with his own plate.

"What are you up to today?" Cassie asked.

"I have a lot to do on the farm, that's why I wanted to make you breakfast, so we could spend some time together." Sebastian sipped his coffee, then set the mug down. "I know that you and Tessa will want to get the murder all figured out."

"Yes, we do. Lucky we had your help." Cassie met his eyes. "If it wasn't for you and Stephanie, we might not have ever had the chance to speak to Devon."

"I didn't do much?" Sebastian ran his hand

through his blond hair. "Ollie sent me a lengthy text about how I put myself and Stephanie at risk by stopping Devon from leaving."

"And I bet he would have been pretty upset if Devon had been able to split town before he had the chance to question him. Sebastian, you might have caught Nancy's killer. Either way, you made sure a criminal didn't get away."

A swift knock at the front door preceded the door swinging open.

"Morning!" Tessa sniffed the air as she walked into the kitchen. "Is that bacon I smell?"

Sebastian laughed. "Of course I made extra for you, Tessa. I knew you'd be over."

"There's coffee, too." Cassie handed her a cup of coffee.

"Thanks." Tessa ate her breakfast as Sebastian and Cassie cleaned up. "I want to try and see Sally at her house." She glanced at the clock on the wall. "We should go soon. She might leave for the farm early and I don't want to miss her. I prefer to speak to her away from the farm. I think we might get more out of her that way."

"Okay. You finish your breakfast, then we'll go." Cassie dried the last of the dishes. "I just have to grab my purse." She walked toward the bedroom. As she slung her purse over her shoulder, she caught her reflection in a mirror. She froze at the sight of the lines on her face and the hint of gray in her hair. Yes, time had a way of passing by without her even noticing it. For Nancy, an entire lifetime had passed her by, until it showed up at her front door when she probably least expected it.

Cassie wondered how Nancy felt when she saw Nina for the first time after all these years. Did she know she was her daughter? Did she long for her for all those years?

"We'd better get going," Tessa called out.

"Be right out." Cassie tucked her hair back behind her ears in an attempt to hide the gray and smoothed down her blouse. She looked in the mirror one last time, then walked into the kitchen.

"I also have to get going." Sebastian smiled as she stepped toward him. "I'll see you later."

"I have a shift later this morning, remember." Cassie gave him a quick kiss.

"Anytime now!" Tessa rapped her knuckles on the front door as she waited for Cassie. "Daylight is burning!"

"I'd better go." Cassie laughed as she walked away. "Okay." She met Tessa at the door. "Let's go!"

"Finally!" Tessa huffed, then led the way through the door and out to the jeep.

As Cassie reached the passenger side, she noticed the goats sulking in Tessa's backyard.

"What's going on with them? They're not even looking for treats."

"Oh, Harry let them have it. They cornered a squirrel in one of their houses. The poor thing was terrified. Harry is usually the one chasing squirrels, but he's never caught one and he actually rescued this one." Tessa opened the jeep door.

"But they wouldn't have hurt the squirrel, right?" Cassie settled in the passenger seat.

"No, although nothing would surprise me with the way those two eat." Tessa started the jeep. "Now they're pouting."

"Harry did a good job." Cassie smiled as Tessa backed out of the driveway.

CHAPTER 13

"I presume you spoke to Mark last night." Cassie glanced over at Tessa. "So, what did he have to say about the murder?"

"Quite a bit." Tessa turned onto the main road. "I didn't realize that adoptions could be so different depending on what state it's in, and how the parents decide to do things. He also said the lawyer for Nancy's estate will want to verify Nina's identity. So, if there's any truth to what Devon said about Nina not really being Nancy's daughter, we'll find out about it. I'm sure that Ollie will question her, that is if he hasn't already." She turned down a side street. "What I wonder is, if Nina isn't really Nina, what is she doing here? Why would she pretend to be someone's daughter? What's the benefit for her?"

"Well, Nancy did leave everything to her. Maybe she thought if she could keep the con going long enough, she would get at least some things out of it. Maybe Nancy figured it out, and that's why Nina killed her. It would explain why they were screaming at each other earlier that morning." Cassie shook her head. "But I don't know why Nancy would continue to let her participate in the holiday celebration if she suspected that she was lying to her."

"Maybe to keep things smooth? Or maybe she really wasn't sure. Devon said he never had the chance to tell Nancy the truth, but maybe someone else did. Someone who had been cautious of Nina from the very beginning. Someone like Sally." Tessa raised an eyebrow as she looked over at Cassie. "It would explain a lot."

"So, if Sally went to Nancy with the truth about Nina, then Nancy confronted Nina, maybe Nina killed her." Cassie bit into her bottom lip. "But if that's true, she's probably worried about who told Nancy the truth, if it even is the truth."

"Which means that Sally might be in danger. Devon is safe for the moment. Last I heard, he's still in custody. But we know already that Nina suspects Sally of disliking her. She might have guessed that she was the one who told Nancy the truth. Or maybe Nancy even told Nina that Sally told her." Tessa turned into a narrow driveway. "This is Sally's house. There's a car in the driveway. I hope she's actually home."

"Only one way to find out." Cassie climbed out of the car and walked up to the front door with Tessa a few steps behind her. She reached up and knocked.

"Get out of here!" Sally glared at them both. "Get off my property! I won't tell you again! The next time I see one of you vultures out here, I'll get my gun!"

Cassie gasped as she took a step back.

Tessa held up her hands as Sally smacked her hand against the doorframe. "We're not reporters, Sally. I'm sure you're getting all kinds of calls today. But that's not why we're here. You know who I am. Tessa. You know I'm not a reporter."

"You're police, then?" Sally eyed Tessa for a moment. "Yes, that's right. I know you used to be on the police force, and I saw you working with the police, yesterday."

"I'm not technically police, anymore. I'm retired." Tessa smiled.

"Oh, I remember you now." Sally squinted. "Sorry, everything has been so stressful."

"I understand." Tessa tipped her head toward Cassie. "This is my friend Cassie. We're here because we want to help you. We're trying to figure out what happened to Nancy."

"I can tell you that. Someone killed her. What else do you need to know?" Sally crossed her arms.

"Who did it?" Cassie spoke up. "Don't you want to know that?"

"Of course I do." Sally gestured for the two of them to step inside. "But the more I tell the police, the more eager they seem to be to point the finger at me. Me! Can you believe that? As if I would kill my own sister." She dropped down into an easy chair and looked up at the ceiling. "Ever since Nancy was killed, I've been trying to figure out who might have done it. I have my suspicions, of course, but no evidence to back it up."

"Who do you suspect?" Cassie sat down on the couch across from her.

Tessa began walking around the living room. Her gaze swept over the pictures on the wall, and the various bouquets of flowers in vases around the room.

"People keep sending flowers." Sally shook her

head. "It's kind, I know. But I hate getting up to answer the door." She ran her hands across her face, then continued. "Look, I don't really know who did it. But I do know that Nina was up to no good."

"No good, how?" Tessa turned to face her. "She's just lost her mother. Don't you want to support her?"

"No. Sorry, if that makes me a monster, so be it. I haven't liked her from the very first moment she arrived here. I don't trust her, and I've told her that. I told my sister that, too, but of course she wouldn't listen to me."

"It would have been hard for her to turn away her child, don't you think?" Cassie raised her eyebrows.

"Not really, no. Look, I never even knew that my sister was pregnant. We weren't very close back then. As far as I knew, she just went on a long vacation."

"She never told you? Even after all these years?" Tessa sat down beside Cassie.

"No, she never said a word about it." Sally sighed. "When Nina showed up, Nancy said that she didn't tell anyone because she didn't want to risk anything interfering with Nina's life. She said she tried very hard to make sure that Nina ended up with a good family who would take good care of her."

"And did she?" Cassie smiled. "Did she have a good life?"

"According to Nina, she was well cared for. But she never felt connected with her family. When they told her that she was adopted, she was eager to find Nancy. At least, that's the story she told." Sally scrunched up her nose. "It never smelled right to me."

"Why do you think she showed up?" Tessa asked.

"I think she discovered that Nancy was an easy mark. She saw everything that my sister had, and she decided she deserved a piece of it." Sally pursed her lips. "But she didn't. My sister placed her up for adoption. She moved on with her life. Nina had her own life, a good one. Then she just decides to show up and demand more? It wasn't fair to Nancy to have such old wounds ripped open again. I told her that. But Nina said it wasn't fair for me to try to keep her from her mother. Her mother? They barely knew each other. I mean Nancy didn't even get her to have a DNA test. She didn't even know if she was really her daughter. She said she believed her and that's all that matters."

"Did you know that they had an argument yesterday morning? Did you happen to be nearby when they started shouting at each other?" Tessa held her gaze.

"What? No. Are you sure about that? I didn't notice any issues between them when we were out together the night before. They were getting along great. It made me sick."

"You were out together? To celebrate something?" Cassie scooted forward on the couch.

"No, just to blow off some steam before the big event. It was at one of those places where you get to throw axes. Do you know what I mean?" Sally looked between them. "Nina suggested it. Apparently she's done it quite a few times before. I thought it would be boring, but it was actually a lot of fun."

"Just the three of you, then?" Tessa asked.

"No, Marie was there, too. She was a bit quiet. But I guess that's because she doesn't like to drink. She stayed sober and had the best throw out of all of us. Not that it was a competition or anything. It was just a bit of fun." Sally pressed her hand to her chest and sank back into her chair. "It's hard to believe that Nancy is gone. She was having so much fun. I kept my mouth shut about Nina, just because I didn't want to ruin it." Tears welled up in her eyes. "I'm sorry, I really can't talk about this anymore. You both should go."

"Sure, we'll see ourselves out." Cassie stood up. "I'm very sorry for your loss, Sally. I hope that it will give you some comfort if they're able to find out who took your sister from you."

"Maybe it will. Who knows?" Sally sniffled.

Tessa stepped out through the front door. Once Cassie closed it behind them, Tessa turned to face her.

"Well, we know that Sally is lying through her teeth, don't we?"

CHAPTER 14

"Why do you say that?" Cassie followed her to the jeep. "What is Sally lying about?"

"She claims that she didn't know about the baby, but Mirabel said that she overheard Nancy and Sally arguing about the pregnancy at the diner all those years ago. She's a bit more reliable than Sally, don't you think?" Tessa jerked open the door of the jeep. "But why would Sally be lying about it?"

"I'm not sure." Cassie sat down in the passenger seat as she tried to imagine herself in Sally's shoes. "Sally just lost her sister. She's not a fan of her sister's long-lost daughter, who's inheriting all of her sister's wealth. Maybe Sally just doesn't want to admit to knowing? Maybe she doesn't want Nina to know that she knew about her?"

"Maybe." Tessa started the jeep. "Maybe it doesn't matter at all, but it does tell me that Sally can't be trusted. Suppose she did discover that Nancy had changed the will before she was killed. Maybe she flew into a rage about it and just killed her. Maybe she didn't have a plan."

"That would make sense." Cassie glanced at the time on the dashboard clock. "I'm going to be late for my shift. Would you mind dropping me off at the diner?"

"No problem. I'm going to make some calls. I want to know a little bit more about Sally and her history with her sister. I might have some friends that can give me a few more details." Tessa turned into the parking lot of the diner. "If you come across any juicy tidbits, let me know."

"I will. I'll come over after I finish. I'm only covering until after lunch." Cassie waved to her, then ran toward the diner. She made it inside just before the minute hand on the large clock on the wall clicked forward another minute to the time her shift was meant to start.

"Cassie! I'm on my way out!" Mirabel waved to her as she headed for the door.

"Sorry I'm late!" Cassie waved back to her.

"You're not late! You're right on time!" Mirabel laughed and blew her a kiss as she closed the door behind her.

Cassie rushed to clock in, stow her purse, and grab her apron. As she served a steady stream of customers, she was distracted from thinking about Nancy's murder. She enjoyed hearing the stories of the residents and visitors of Little Leaf Creek and making sure they had a great experience at the diner.

Cassie looked up to see the door swing open and Marie, Nancy's friend, step inside

"Coffee, please?" Marie sat down at the front counter and plunked a large purse down on the empty stool beside her.

"Hi, Marie." Cassie smiled at her as she grabbed a mug and a pot of coffee. She poured coffee into the mug, then set it down in front of her. She slid a selection of sweeteners closer to her. "Would you like cream?"

"Yes, please, and something sweet." Marie fiddled with her mug. "I need a pick-me-up."

"Sure." Cassie grabbed coffee creamer from the fridge behind the counter and poured some into Marie's mug. "How about a piece of apple pie?"

"Perfect." Marie smiled.

"I'm so sorry about your friend, Marie." Cassie grabbed a plate.

"Thanks. That's what everyone keeps saying to me." Marie stared down into the mug and continued to fiddle with the handle. "And I appreciate it, definitely, but what does it even mean?" She looked up at Cassie.

"What does it mean?" Cassie's voice softened as she noticed the sadness in the woman's eyes. "I guess it's one of those things you say when you know there's nothing you can say that will make it better." She placed the piece of pie in front of her.

"Maybe there is something you can say that will make it better." Marie stared into Cassie's eyes. "Did you figure it out, yet?"

"Figure it out?" Cassie stared back at her.

"Who killed Nancy?"

Cassie's heart skipped a beat. "The police are conducting a thorough investigation."

"And so are you. I've heard all about the questioning you and Tessa have been doing. I thought maybe you'd already come to a conclusion."

"Not yet, no." Cassie bit into her bottom lip.

"But you must have some good suspects, right?" Marie tapped a sugar packet against the counter.

"Not really. It might have even been someone from out of town." Cassie didn't want to highlight anyone as a suspect and influence anything that Marie might tell her. "Do you have any suspects?"

"Just the usual ones. There's Kevin, of course. I warned Nancy not to treat him so badly after the trees were stolen. I told her that people make mistakes, and it's best to be forgiving, especially around this time of year." Marie ripped the sugar packet open and poured the contents into her coffee. "But she said that men try to take advantage of women who are in charge. She insisted she needed to show him that she wasn't a pushover. So she did."

"Is that why she was following Devon? To prove to him that she wasn't a pushover?" Cassie handed her a spoon to stir her coffee with.

"I warned her about that, too. I said to her, what do you think he's going to do when he catches you following him around? People are very protective of their secrets, you know. It's always best to let them have them." Marie stirred her coffee, then set the spoon down on the plate beside the pie. "I don't know why I wasted my breath. She never listened to me."

"Never?" Cassie paused to greet a few customers who entered the diner, then looked back at Marie.

"Is that why you didn't know about Nina? She didn't tell you about the pregnancy?"

"I had no idea." Marie's lips tightened. "I thought we were very close. I thought we told each other everything. She confided in me about how jealous she was of Sally. She always thought Sally was much prettier than her and had a much easier time in life. I told her all about the troubles in my marriage. I really thought we were close."

"It sounds like you were. Maybe she had a good reason for not telling you about the baby."

"I'm sure she did, but I don't know what it was. I was hurt at first, when Nina showed up. But then I made it my goal to make Nina feel like family." Marie smiled. "If she's Nancy's daughter, then I wanted her to be like a niece to me."

"That's very sweet of you. I guess you're a very forgiving person. Excuse me for a moment." Cassie hurried over to a table and offered to take their order. Once she'd done so and delivered the order to the kitchen, she returned to Marie.

"You know, Cassie, it's like this." Marie finished the last sip of her coffee, then placed some money on the counter. "You can have expectations of people, you can think you know who they are, but they will always surprise you. You can't control that. So, your choice is to either accept them for who they are, or move on with your life." She stood up from the stool. "Thanks for the coffee and pie."

"Let me get you your change." Cassie picked up the money.

"No, thanks, no change needed. I'm going to see about the flowers for Nancy's funeral. Sally refuses to help. I guess because Nancy left her nothing. Nina is so upset about everything that she doesn't want to leave the house unless she has to. So, it's up to me. I just hope that I pick out the right ones. Probably something yellow. Nancy always loved yellow." Marie offered Cassie a sad smile, then walked toward the door.

As Cassie watched Marie leave, she hoped the murder would be solved soon and bring those close to Nancy some closure.

CHAPTER 15

With Cassie at work for the rest of the morning, Tessa had spent a little time making calls to see if she could find any leads as to who Nina's father was, and why Sally might be lying. However, each call had led to yet another dead end. She turned her attention to making cookies instead.

As Tessa began to relax, and her thoughts cleared, she ran through the suspects in her mind. Kevin was furious over his lost paycheck and all the damage that would do to his family.

A swift knock on the door drew her from her thoughts. She recognized the sound of his knock.

"Go away, Mark!"

"Tessa, I'm not leaving until you open the door."

Mark's booming voice held a hint of amusement and a large amount of determination.

"I'm working, Mark." Tessa finished mixing the frosting and set the mixer down on the counter. She wiped her hand on a towel, then turned toward the front door. "I don't have time to talk right now."

"You offered to let me help, remember?" Mark called through the door.

"All right, fine. Come inside, it's not like it's locked." Tessa picked up the bowl of frosting and carried it over to the waiting tray of cookies.

"It smells delicious in here." Mark stepped into the kitchen. "Did you make more cookies?"

"Can never have enough for the little ones." Tessa glanced up at him. "What are you wearing?" She looked over his bright red suit with large, golden buttons.

"It's part of my Santa Claus costume. I'm going to the children's charity to hand out gifts today, then I'm wearing it for the Christmas parade tomorrow. I'm part of the parade." Mark grinned. "Do you like it?" He did a slow spin in front of her. "It's a little snug, I know. I guess I put on a few pounds this year."

"It's fine. I'm sure the kids will love it."

"Thanks." Mark attempted to stick a fingertip into the bowl of frosting.

"No, you don't." Tessa pulled the bowl away. "You'll get your germs in it."

"My germs?" Mark laughed as he leaned against the counter beside her.

"Things have to stay sanitary in my kitchen." Tessa clucked her tongue as she began spreading some frosting over a large sleigh-shaped cookie.

"You mean when the goats aren't in it?" Mark pointed down to the cuff of one of his pant legs. "Gerry took a bite out of me."

"Oh, they're both so riled up." Tessa eyed the bottom of his pants. "I'm sure we can find someone to fix it. I'll pay for it, of course."

"It's fine. It's not that bad." Mark turned on the sink faucet and began washing his hands. "I'm here to work, remember?"

"Well, while you work, maybe you can help me figure something out." Tessa handed him a small spatula and directed him toward a tray of Christmas tree-shaped cookies.

"Sure. I've been wanting to talk about this, too. You see, you're so good at being alone, the thought of taking a chance on inviting someone into your life, it scares you." Mark softened his voice. "It's nothing to be ashamed of, Tessa. Everyone gets scared sometimes."

"Oh, stop it." Tessa swung her spatula toward him, which caused some of the frosting on it to fling off and land on his cheek.

"Hey!" Mark laughed as he swept his finger through the frosting, then licked it off. "Yes, it's as good as I knew it would be!"

"I want to frost cookies and talk about the murder, that's all."

"All right, Tessa. Let's talk about the murder." Mark washed his hands again. "What's on your mind?"

"Sally." Tessa turned her attention back to the cookies. "Cassie and I spoke to her this morning, and she lied to me."

"About?" Mark spread green frosting across a tree-shaped cookie.

"She claimed she didn't know that Nancy was pregnant. But Mirabel witnessed an argument between the two of them, when Nancy must have been pregnant, that indicated Sally did know." Tessa set down her spatula and turned to look at him. "So, why would she lie about that?"

"Probably because she thought that admitting to knowing about the baby would paint her in a bad light somehow." Mark continued on to another cookie. "But I'm not sure how. Knowing about the baby shouldn't be a big deal, right? Unless she promised to keep Nancy's secret, and she feels like even if she talks about it now she's betraying her. Or maybe there's someone she didn't want to find out."

"That's true. Maybe she didn't keep the secret just for her sister. Maybe she benefited in some way from keeping it."

"Figuring out how, might give you a good clue as to what led to Nancy's death." Mark reached for one of the cookies on her tray. "That one looks a little broken, guess I'll have to eat it."

"Don't you dare!" Tessa smacked the back of his hand with her spatula, which sent frosting flying through the air at both of them. A big splotch landed on Mark's jacket.

"All right, that's it!" Mark chuckled as he dug his spatula in for a big scoop of green frosting. "There's only so much I can take."

"What are you doing?" Tessa stared at him, her eyes wide as she backed away.

"Tessa, you can't expect me not to fight back." Mark waved the frosting-laden spatula through the air as he grinned.

"Mark, don't do it!" Tessa's voice raised. "We're not kids! We're in our sixties!"

"Speak for yourself. I have been steadily regressing since I turned fifty." Mark laughed as he raised the spatula in the air. "Time for payback."

"Mark!" Tessa shrieked as he flung the frosting off the spatula.

A large splatter of green frosting smacked Tessa right across the nose and dripped down toward her mouth.

"Unbelievable!" She thought about throwing him out of her house. But his quiet giggle followed by another splash of frosting on her cheek caused her own lips to twitch. "Stop!" She grabbed a handful of frosting from her bowl and threw it straight at him.

"Not my hair, Tessa!" Mark gasped as he laughed. He pulled some of the frosting out of his hair, then reached for Tessa's shoulder and arm.

"Don't you dare! Stay away from me!" Tessa shrieked as she ran toward the other side of the kitchen.

"Tessa! Are you okay?" Cassie burst through the front door, just as a dollop of frosting struck Tessa on the forehead.

Cassie's heart raced. The scream she'd heard

from outside the door made her think that the killer was inside with Tessa. Instead, she walked into the strangest scene she'd ever witnessed in Tessa's kitchen.

Stunned by the mess, and Mark's bright red suit, she didn't notice the goats on the front porch until they rushed past her, into the house.

"Oh no!" Cassie lunged for Gerry in an attempt to keep him out of the kitchen.

Gerry skipped right past her and ran toward Tessa.

Billy had the same idea. His tongue lolled out of his mouth as he sniffed the sugar in the air.

"Stop!" Tessa demanded as the goats swarmed her in search of a delicious treat.

Gerry launched himself straight for Tessa with a flying leap.

"Tessa, look out!" Cassie shouted.

Tessa dodged out of the way.

Mark grabbed her arm to steady her.

"I'm so sorry!" Cassie picked up one of the cookies and waved it in front of the goats. "Here, do you want a treat?" She flinched as they bolted toward her. After a quick dodge, she swung open the back door and threw the cookie outside.

The goats tried to climb over each other in an

attempt to get to the door first. As they stumbled through it, Cassie pushed the door closed behind them.

"What's going on in here?" Cassie laughed as she swept her gaze around the kitchen. "It looks like I missed a fun morning."

"It was fun." Mark laughed.

"Well, I still have plenty of cookies left to frost." Tessa wiped the frosting from her shirt.

"I actually have to get going." Mark grabbed a towel and wiped some of the frosting off his face. "Thanks for a fun morning." He smiled as he stepped away from the kitchen counter. "Good luck, Cassie, she's probably going to put you to work."

"He's not wrong. Let's talk and frost at the same time." Tessa wiped down the counter. "I have to whip up some more frosting."

"Oh, did you run out during your little food fight?" Cassie smiled as she picked up one of the empty bowls.

"Let's not waste our time talking about that." Tessa turned toward the mixing bowl. "Let's try and solve this murder."

"I still think that Nina might not be who she says she is." Cassie grabbed a spatula. She placed her notebook beside her, so she could consult her notes if necessary.

"I agree." Tessa turned on the mixer and mixed the sugar and butter together. "I spoke to a contact at the station, and apparently Devon is still in custody."

"Devon said Nancy was harassing him." Cassie glanced at her notebook. "Maybe he knew she was following him and taking pictures, trying to catch him."

"It would explain why she never managed to catch him in the act of cutting down the trees and couldn't find any proof that would lead to him being arrested." Tessa peeked at Cassie's notebook. "So why would Devon kill Nancy?"

"Maybe he confronted her about the pictures. Maybe he's afraid of going to prison? Maybe he's afraid of losing his illegal income?" Cassie put some frosting on her spatula. "If Devon knew about Nancy following him and taking the pictures, maybe someone tipped him off. Maybe it was Nina?"

"Why would she do that to her mother?" Tessa added a few drops of food coloring to some of the frosting. "How would it benefit her to betray Nancy like that?"

"I don't know, but maybe if Nina was tipping

him off, and Nancy found out about it, that might give Nina more of a motive to kill her mother. I'm sure Nancy would have written her out of the will, and maybe even refused to have anything to do with her, if she knew that Nina was protecting Devon, no matter the reason." Cassie put down the spatula and added a note to her notebook.

"I think we need to speak to Nina again. If we just have a casual conversation with her, she might let it slip."

"Good idea."

CHAPTER 16

"I think we're getting close, don't you?" Cassie looked toward the entrance of Nancy's farm as the jeep neared it. "Things don't quite make sense, yet, but something is definitely there to find."

"Yes, I think so, too. It's clear that Sally is hiding something, and now it's very likely that Nina is, too." Tessa whistled as she pulled into the driveway and noticed a couple of trucks lined up along it. "Interesting." She parked the jeep as she swept her gaze toward the trucks.

"Those are big trucks." Cassie narrowed her eyes. "What is Nina up to?"

"Let's find out." Tessa stepped out of the jeep with tension flowing through her movements.

Cassie followed after her, fascinated by the sudden shift in her friend. One moment she could be arguing with her about a frosting fight, and the next she looked completely focused, determined to find out the truth.

"Excuse me, sir, we're looking for Nina." Tessa stepped in front of a burly man in coveralls, carrying a large lamp.

"She's up there in one of the rockers." He tipped his head toward the sprawling front porch.

"Thanks." Tessa eyed the lamp.

"It looks antique." Cassie watched the man load it onto a nearby truck.

"It sure does. I guess Nina isn't wasting any time, is she?" Tessa's lips tightened as she approached the front porch. "I mean, Nancy's estate wouldn't have been settled, yet."

Cassie watched two men carry a small couch toward the other truck.

"Nina?" Tessa stepped up onto the porch.

"Yes?" Nina rocked forward in her chair. "Is there something I can help you with?"

"It looks like we might need to be the ones offering help." Cassie smiled slightly as she stepped up onto the porch as well. "You seem to have a big task to handle."

"I do, but I think I have enough help." Nina tightened her coat around her. "They told me they could do it in two hours, but it's already been three."

"What exactly are they doing?" Tessa raised her eyebrows. "Are you moving already?"

"No, of course not." Nina forced a laugh. "You see, my mother was a bit of a pack rat. I want to host a special ceremony to honor her, in her home, but there just isn't enough room with all of this junk. So, I'm having it moved to storage. It'll make things easier to deal with later, too."

"Then you're planning on moving?" Cassie sat down in a rocking chair beside her.

"Well, it's not exactly like I ever actually lived here. I was staying here for a little while, so that I could get to know my mother a little better. Now, I can't do that." Nina sat back in her chair as she picked up a cup of coffee. "So, what's the point?"

"I'm sure being surrounded by her things might give you some insight into the person that she was." Tessa watched as more items were carried out to the trucks. "That might be hard to do if they're all locked away somewhere, though."

"Trust me, this is just a small portion of what is filling up that house. But I'm sure you didn't just stop by for a friendly visit. What's on your mind?" Nina looked between the two of them.

"Actually, I'd like to know why you were telling Devon about your mother's plans to get proof of his trespassing, stealing the trees, and possibly having him arrested." Tessa's voice hardened as she locked eyes with Nina.

Nina choked on a sip of her coffee. Her hand trembled as she set the cup back down. She cleared her throat, then stared down at the wooden slats of the porch.

"How do you know about that? Did Devon tell you?"

"So, it's true?" Cassie shifted closer to her. "Were you and Devon dating? Is that why you put your mother at risk?"

"No way." Nina sighed. "You have it all wrong. I know it looks bad, but I was trying to protect her."

"Protect her, by making her the target of a possible killer? How could you betray her and put her in danger like that?" Tessa narrowed her eyes. "Yes, that does look very bad."

"I was trying to protect her from a possible killer. After Devon caught my mother following him, he started sending her threats. Nothing that we could go to the police with, but still scary. I begged her to stop following him because I had no idea what he might do if he caught her again. But she refused to stop. She insisted that it was her duty to protect the trees, and to stop him. So, I contacted Devon myself. I told him that if he promised not to hurt my mother, I would warn him when she told me she planned to follow him. That way, he could make sure that he didn't get caught doing anything illegal. I felt like it was the only way that I could keep her safe." Tears slid down Nina's cheeks as she shook her head. "But apparently, he didn't honor that promise. He must have gotten fed up with her and decided he was going to get rid of her once and for all."

"We don't know that, yet, for sure." Tessa studied Nina. "You should have gone to the police, if you really thought Devon was a danger to your mother."

"I wanted to, but I wasn't sure if it would make things worse. I swear, I was only trying to keep her safe. I tried to warn her. I tried to reason with her. I got so upset that we fought about it, and when I told her how scared I was she would get hurt, she told me that wasn't her problem. I lost my temper, because I had finally found her, and all she cared about was catching Devon. I told her, if she went near him again, I would kill her." Nina grimaced. "But, of course, I didn't mean that. I just wanted to protect her."

"What are you doing?" A shrill scream came from the middle of the driveway. "Put that down this instant!" The scream grew louder. "Those are my sister's things. You can't just take them."

"Oh no!" Nina groaned as she stood up. "Aunt Sally, please calm down!"

"I will not calm down." Sally charged toward the porch. "You don't have any right to throw out all of Nancy's things."

"Sally." Marie ran up behind her. Despite her usually quiet demeanor, her voice raised higher and higher as she reached the porch. "Sally, stop this right now. You know Nancy wouldn't approve of you yelling at Nina like this. You're acting crazy."

"Nancy wouldn't approve?" Sally spun around to face her. "I'll tell you what she wouldn't approve of, she wouldn't approve of all of her things being tossed out of her house before her body is even in the ground!"

"I'm not tossing anything out!" Nina put her hands on her hips. "Stop being so dramatic. I'm just trying to make the house look nice so we can have a beautiful service for her. Don't you think she deserves that?"

"Of course she does." Marie clasped her hands together in front of her. "I'd be happy to help in any way I can, Nina."

"You can help by moving all of Nancy's things back into the house." Sally swung her arms through the air. "Am I the only one thinking straight around here? Oh, Nancy." She sank down onto the top step of the porch. "If only you were here. If only you could see this. You would know I was right about everything." She stared up at the sky. "Do you see it now? Do you see that she's just a con artist out to take everything from you?"

"That's enough, Sally." Marie grasped her shoulder. "You're making an upsetting time even more difficult."

"Why would she do this? Why would she leave anything to her?" Sally's words dissolved into tears as she began to sob.

"This is ridiculous," Nina snapped. "If you want to have a tantrum, you'd better have it somewhere else, or I'll call the police and have you removed."

"Nina!" Marie glared at her. "She's just lost her sister! We both did. Didn't we, Sally?" She pulled her to her feet and looked into her eyes. "But we still have each other. We've known each other for a long time. We can get through this together."

"What's the point?" Sally pulled away from her and began to wander down the driveway. "It won't bring her back."

Marie followed after her.

"Sally's really upset." Cassie glanced over at Tessa.

"She's a great actress is what she is." Nina shook her head as she jerked the door open to the house. "Don't let her fool you. One minute she's saying she won't attend a memorial for her sister because her sister didn't bother to leave her anything, and the next minute she's bawling her eyes out claiming she's so heartbroken. I'm just glad my mother never had to see this." She stepped inside and closed the door behind her.

"What a mess." Tessa walked toward the jeep. "All of this anger makes me wonder if they'll ever move on."

"I think Sally has a right to be angry." Cassie

pulled open the passenger door. "Nina could have checked with her before she started moving everything around."

"True." Tessa climbed into the driver's seat. "But she owns everything, or at least she will once the estate is settled, and like she said, she's just storing it, not getting rid of it."

"Maybe." Cassie buckled her seat belt. "But I would be upset if someone started going through my loved one's things, especially so soon after they passed away, even if it was to go into storage. Sally certainly knows what Nancy would want more than Nina, they barely knew each other."

"Sure, they hadn't known each other long, but maybe they felt an instant connection." Tessa started the jeep. "None of that really matters. What matters is who killed Nancy. Right now, Devon is in custody. He's Ollie's prime suspect. He's not going to let us anywhere near him. So, all we can do is feed him the information that we've found." She turned onto the highway that headed toward Rombsby. "I can tell you one thing that concerns me, all of those items being moved out of the house. If we had any chance of still discovering where the murderer's clothes might be, it might have disappeared with those moving trucks."

"That's true." Cassie narrowed her eyes as Tessa exited the highway. "If the killer changed their clothes after the murder, couldn't we narrow down our suspects by figuring out who might have changed?"

"There were so many people there. I don't think too many were paying attention to what other people were wearing. And there's still the possibility the killer took off their coat before the murder, then put it back on after, which would explain how they could have walked out of there without ever changing."

"That would indicate that the killer had been planning this. Which means it was likely someone fairly close to Nancy. I still think it's possible that Nina is behind it all. She just lost her mother, but she's so quick to empty out her house?" Cassie peered through the windshield. "That feels strange to me. When my husband died, even though we hadn't been very close for a long time, I couldn't even throw out his toothbrush. Everything seemed to carry a bit of sacredness to it. It was a struggle when it came time to pack things up."

"I'm sure it was." Tessa turned down another side road. "But maybe it's different for Nina. She never grew up living with Nancy. Maybe seeing her mother's things meant nothing to her. Or maybe the grief of seeing her mother's things is too overwhelming for her."

"Maybe." Cassie looked through the windshield. "Where are you going? This isn't the way back to Little Leaf Creek."

"No, it's not. I have a hunch. I want to speak to Kevin again. I want to find out more about his relationship with Nancy." Tessa slowed down as she neared a small apartment building.

"Do you really think he might have killed her over a paycheck?" Cassie looked over the unkept grounds of the complex as Tessa turned into it.

"I think he was already on the edge of a breakdown, between his divorce, missing his children, and his financial strain. It wouldn't be the first time that someone snapped over finances." Tessa parked in the first empty spot, then turned the engine off. "It might not have been just about the money, but the fact that Nancy was so quick to blame him. If he felt they had a more personal relationship, for her to suddenly cut him out of her life, might have really hurt his ego." She opened the car door. "Like I said, it's just a hunch." She stepped out of the jeep. "Maybe this will lead to nothing, or maybe it will lead to something."

"There's his truck." Cassie pointed to a pickup truck parked in front of a small apartment. "That must be his place."

"Good, then he's probably home." As Tessa walked toward the door, it swung open.

Kevin stood in the doorway.

"We just wanted to have a quick chat." Tessa smiled.

"It's all right, you can come in." Kevin stepped back from the door and watched them both as they stepped inside. "I don't have anything to hide."

"Thanks." Cassie glanced around the small living room she stepped into. Aside from a few piles of toys in one corner, she saw no indication that children lived there. The apartment appeared to have a single bedroom. A small wooden table took up most of the kitchen.

"It's good that you're being so cooperative, Kevin." Tessa strolled toward the kitchen. "Do you mind if I get myself a glass of water? I'm so thirsty."

"Let me get it for you." Kevin hurried past her and opened one of the cabinets. "I'll make sure I have a clean glass for you. Sorry, I'm not really used to having guests." He grabbed a glass from the cabinet and pointed out the dishes in the sink. "I'm not great at keeping up with the chores."

"That's all right, you don't have to impress us." Cassie studied the pictures on the wall. Two kids smiled from different frames. A few of the pictures featured a tall, blonde woman as well. Kevin's image didn't appear in any of them. "Are these your kids?"

"Yes. And their mother." Kevin handed Tessa a glass of water. "Cute kids, right?"

"Very." Cassie smiled.

"Luckily, they took after their mother." Kevin grinned. "But my oldest, my son, Bryce, he has my strong arm for pitching. He's a star on his Little League team."

"That's great. You must love going to his games." Cassie turned to look at him.

"Actually, I don't get to see him play too often. I'm usually working. But his mother records the games for me sometimes." Kevin leaned against the kitchen counter. "It's not the same, I know. But it's the best I can do right now. At least she might let me take them to the Christmas parade this year. I won't be working for once."

"It seems like you work very hard to make sure your children are taken care of." Tessa set the glass down on the counter beside him. She was tempted to mention the money he wasted at the bar but knew that would only upset him. She wouldn't be able to get information from him that way. "Did they ever visit the farm with you? Did they meet Nancy?"

"She invited them to visit, yes. I brought them one time, and they loved seeing all of the different trees. Nancy even gave them a tour herself. They really liked her." Kevin shook his head. "I haven't told them what happened, yet."

"It sounds like you and Nancy knew each other pretty well." Cassie met his eyes. "Were you friends?"

"I thought we were." Kevin cringed. "But when the trees were stolen, everything changed."

"It must have been infuriating for her to turn on you like that." Tessa froze as a strange chirping sound emitted from behind a door. "What's that?"

"Oh. Nothing." Kevin coughed.

"I hear it, too." Cassie looked toward the sound. "Is that a bird? Do you have a pet?"

"Please don't tell anyone. I'm not supposed to have any pets. But my kids saw this bird at the pet store and begged me for him. I figured, what harm could a bird do? Right?" Kevin opened the door to his bedroom.

A few piles of dirty clothes were scattered across the thick carpet. Near the only large window, a bird cage stood. Inside, a bright yellow canary fluttered from perch to perch and chirped.

"Oh wow, he's so beautiful!" Cassie smiled at the sight of the bird. "Can I take a closer look?"

"Sure." Kevin nodded. "He's pretty friendly. Just don't stick your finger in the cage or he might nip you."

"Thanks." Cassie glanced back over her shoulder as Tessa continued to ask Kevin about his relationship with Nancy. Cassie walked closer to the cage, crouched down and plucked a yellow feather from the floor. She tucked it into her pocket, then stepped back out of the bedroom. "Tessa, we should go. We have that meeting, remember?" She tipped her head toward the door.

Tessa stared at her for a moment, then turned toward the door. "Right, of course."

"What was that about?" Tessa followed Cassie to the jeep.

"This." Cassie pulled the feather from her pocket. "Maybe Ollie can try to match it to the one that was found on Nancy's coat. If he can, then it's very likely that Kevin is the one who killed Nancy."

"Clever." Tessa hopped into the jeep and started the engine. "Let's get it over to Ollie and give it to him. Maybe he'll test it. Then I have to get back to the house and make more frosting."

"I'm not surprised, considering what you did with the last batch." Cassie grinned as she settled in her seat.

"Never mind that." Tessa drove down the street.

She turned into the police station, then pulled up close to the front door. "You run it in. I'll wait here."

"Be right back." Cassie jumped out of the jeep and hurried into the police station. The officer behind the receptionist desk contacted Oliver, then directed her toward his office. As she passed by the holding cells, the door that led to them was open, and she noticed Devon inside one of them. He paced back and forth. His hair was ruffled, and he looked agitated.

"Stay away from him, Cassie." Oliver stepped into the hallway before she could go near the holding cell.

"I will." Cassie held out the feather. "I found this at Kevin's place. He has a canary. I thought you might want to try to see if it matches the feather at the crime scene."

"I can, but I can't use it as evidence, even if it is a match. Also, it might be from his canary, but it got onto Nancy's clothes at another time." Oliver tucked it into an evidence bag. "I'd better get back to it."

"Okay." Cassie turned away and accidentally met Devon's eyes.

Devon grabbed the bars of the holding cell and thrust his face toward them. "I didn't do it! I don't care what they say! I didn't kill her!"

Cassie hurried toward the door. As she stepped out of the police station, her skin crawled with an uneasy sensation.

"Everything okay?" Tessa looked over at her as she climbed into the jeep. "You have a worried look on your face."

"I don't know." Cassie sighed as Tessa pulled away from the curb. "Devon is really the best suspect, and he's certainly someone I want to see behind bars, but I feel pushed in a different direction. I don't even know what direction. I have no idea where to start."

"We start at the beginning." Tessa turned out of the parking lot of the police station and toward their street. "Step by step. We start back at the farm, back at the moment that we found Nancy dead."

"Maybe we missed something there?" Cassie looked over at her.

"It's possible." Tessa turned into her driveway.

"No one saw or heard anything, which means that this was likely planned. That would mean this was likely premeditated. In which case, someone planned to murder her with an ax." Cassie stepped out of the jeep as the goats ran up to the fence. She tossed some treats to them.

"Well, Devon's in custody. He seems pretty

ruthless. We also have Kevin to consider, who's in a very desperate situation. Both men are familiar with wielding axes." Tessa unlocked the door and led Cassie inside.

"But from what we can tell, Nina stands to benefit the most from Nancy being dead. And there's Sally, of course. Maybe Nancy told her about the change to the will, and Sally got very angry and lost it and killed her." Cassie sat down at the kitchen table and pulled her notebook out of her purse.

"Maybe." Tessa began lining up ingredients on the counter.

Harry walked into the kitchen and yawned. He stared up at them both with big, brown eyes.

"Oops, sorry, Harry." Tessa filled his food dish. "I didn't forget. I promise." She patted his head as he sniffed the food. "What's wrong? Aren't you hungry?"

He took a few bites of the food, then walked away.

Tessa frowned as she watched him. "That's not like him. I'll have to keep an eye on him."

"No, it isn't. I'll keep an eye on him as well." Cassie frowned. "I've been thinking about why Marie wouldn't have known about Nancy's pregnancy." She sat back in her chair and crossed her legs as she watched Tessa begin frosting the cookies. "What if the reason that Nancy didn't tell her has to do with who the father of the baby was? That's been the biggest part of the secret, right? Nancy refused to tell Nina who her father was, even after accepting her into her home and writing her into her will. It seems odd that she'd be willing to do so much for Nina, but not that one thing she asked for. If Nancy kept her best friend in the dark, maybe it has to do with that?"

"I bet that's it!" Tessa began using a piping tool to decorate another cookie. "That's probably why Sally is denying knowing about the pregnancy, too. Nina's father must have been a very important person, if Nancy tried so hard to hide the truth."

"Important enough to kill over?" Cassie stared down at her list of suspects. "I want to believe that Devon did this. I can believe that Kevin did it. I'm not so sure about Sally. I feel like it would take a lot to kill her own sister."

"Family doesn't always mean the same thing to people. Some would do anything to protect their family. Others barely acknowledge them. Maybe Sally was tired of living in the shadows of her sister's success."

"It's interesting, too, that Nancy never married

or had any other children." Cassie sat back in her chair. "I know not every woman wants to be a mother, but don't you think she would have wanted a partner?"

"Not everyone wants romance, either." Tessa finished frosting the last cookie. "It comes with its own complications. The single life can be a very liberating experience."

"Has it been liberating for you?" Cassie held up one hand. "I know, I'm not supposed to pry. But I'm genuinely curious. I was so young when I got married, and honestly, when my husband died, I never thought I'd be in another relationship, but things happened so fast, and I don't regret it. I love being with Sebastian. I look forward to seeing him and spending time with him, sharing my life with him. Don't you ever want those things?"

"I have them." Tessa leaned back against the counter as she met Cassie's eyes. "With you. Friendship can be just as fulfilling. If you're asking me, do I regret being single most of my life? No, I don't." She smiled. "I've always made my own choices, had my own space, and followed every whim I had. I have Harry, and my goats, and I feel like my life is very full. Too full, sometimes." She cringed at the sound of the goats crashing into something in the backyard. "It's not wrong to want someone in your life, Cassie, but it's not wrong to want to be alone, either. My guess is that Nancy learned she was happier on her own, especially after she went through an unwanted pregnancy with someone she didn't name. She sure made a good life for herself, though, didn't she?"

"I guess she did." Cassie looked back down at her list. "But all of those secrets she kept might be what got her killed."

A loud knock on the door, followed by Harry's bellowing bark, and bleats from the goats, silenced Tessa before she could speak.

CHAPTER 19

"Tessa!" Mark called out from the porch. "Let me in before these goats ruin my outfit."

"The door is open, Mark!" Tessa opened the back door to let Harry out.

Harry bolted through the door and stumbled over a bowl on the back porch.

"Oh, Harry!" Tessa gasped as Harry ran off barking in the direction of the goats. "No wonder he doesn't want to eat. Somehow he got into one of my bowls of frosting!" She snatched up the bowl. "See, Cassie? A very full life." She stepped back into the kitchen.

Mark poked his head in through the front door. "Is it safe?"

"Do you really want me to answer that?" Tessa flashed him a grin. "Or would turning around and running while you still can, seem like a better decision?"

"Trust me, you're going to want to hear what I have to say." Mark stepped farther into the house and closed the door behind him. "I bring them treats, you know, but they still don't like me."

"Must not be the right treats." Cassie looked up at him from the kitchen table. "Or they just really like them and want more."

"Could be." Mark hovered near the door and eyed Tessa with some hesitation.

"Yes, it's safe to come in, Mark." Tessa gestured to a chair in the living room. "But stay out of the kitchen. I finally finished frosting the cookies, and I don't want any surprise food fights breaking out."

"I promise not to go near them. At least not until tomorrow at the parade." Mark sat down in the chair, then looked at Cassie. "I'm glad you're here, too. I ran into Sebastian just before, and he said that he hasn't been able to reach you."

"He hasn't?" Cassie reached into her purse for her phone. Her eyes widened as her fingertips sought the familiar rectangle. "It's not in my purse. I must have lost it somewhere!"

"Don't worry, we can track it down. But first, here's my news." Mark waited for them to sit across from him. "I was able to get some information about Nancy's will from a friend of mine. He confirmed that Nancy had already made the changes to her will, leaving just about everything to Nina. He said he expected the process to be fairly simple, but he's still waiting on some paperwork to verify her identity. I've been running into the same roadblocks. He wants Nina to get a DNA test. She's agreed, but she hasn't gotten one, yet. She says she's still too upset." He ran his hand along the back of his neck. "Something just doesn't feel right."

"Exactly! There's something off about all of this. This whole time we've believed that Sally is the only one who knew about Nancy being pregnant, right?" Cassie stood up and began to pace back and forth. "But we don't know that for sure, do we? Marie was closer to Nancy than Sally was. It just doesn't make sense to me that Nancy would confide in Sally, who she didn't feel very close to, instead of her lifelong best friend."

"That's a good point." Mark tapped his fingertip against the table. "Actually, Nancy left a considerable amount of her wealth to Marie. Nina inherited most of it, but what she didn't leave to Nina, she left to Marie."

"She left money to Marie and not to Sally?" Cassie asked incredulously. "That seems like more than just a lack of closeness. She must have really disliked her sister to leave her out like that."

"Maybe because she was so against Nina being taken in as part of the family." Tessa smacked her hand across her knee. "It might have soured Nancy against Sally."

"Or Nina manipulated Nancy into turning against her sister," Cassie suggested. "If Nina saw Sally as someone who stood in the way of her making a strong connection with her mother, she might have targeted her."

"Actually, you might be right about that. I'm still having a hard time finding anyone who can verify Nina's identity, or anyone who handled her adoption. I haven't been able to track down her adoptive parents, either." Mark clasped his hands together on the table. "Some closed adoptions can be very difficult to trace. I'm going to keep trying, but right now I'm not sure how much more I'll find. A lot of the information is only available to those family members involved in the adoption."

"Then maybe it's time we stopped counting on paperwork and started digging into the people that knew Nancy best. Like Marie." Cassie picked up her purse and checked through it again. "I really need to find my phone."

"Here, let me call you. If it's here, you'll hear it ring." Tessa called Cassie.

"Nothing." Cassie listened for her ringtone. "I wonder where it could be." She watched as Tessa put her phone away. "I need to tell Sebastian I can't find my phone."

"You can use mine to call him and put his mind at ease." Tessa pulled her phone back out of her pocket and handed it to Cassie, then froze as she watched Cassie easily type in the password. "You're right, Cassie. We've only been close friends for a short time, but you know my phone password. I know yours. I've shared things with you about my life that I've never shared with anyone else. Marie and Nancy were lifelong friends. There's no way that Marie doesn't know more than she's saying."

"Exactly." Cassie put the phone to her ear. "Let me just check in with Sebastian, and then I say we head to Marie's before it gets too late."

"I guess that's my cue to leave. I'll let you know

if I turn up anything else." Mark hugged Tessa, then started toward the door.

"Thanks, Mark." Tessa took her phone back from Cassie. "Let's go find some answers." She started toward the front door with Cassie close behind her.

CHAPTER 20

Cassie dug into her purse as Tessa started the jeep.

"I just wish I could find my phone. I have no idea where I might have left it. Sometimes I search and search for it, and it ends up being hidden in here somewhere."

"We'll find it. There's a way to track it with the internet, right?" Tessa turned onto a side road.

"I think so, but I have to have a certain setting turned on for that, and I'm not sure if I did." Cassie closed her eyes and tried to run back through every minute of her day. "It must be at the diner. I know I used it before I started working today, and I don't think I've used it since. I probably just left it there because I was in such a rush to meet up with you."

"Use my phone and call Mirabel. She can see if it's still there." Tessa turned down another road. "We're only a minute or two away from Marie's house, so make it quick."

"I will, thank you." Cassie dialed Mirabel's number, then waited for her to pick up. "Ugh, voicemail." She left a quick message, then set the phone back down in the middle console. "I'm sure she's in the middle of the dinner rush. She'll get back to me as soon as she can. At least I know where it probably is, so I can relax a little."

"Nothing to worry about. We can go to the diner on the way home." Tessa flashed her a smile, then turned into Marie's driveway. "And it looks like Marie is home. Hopefully, she'll be in a talkative mood."

"She's had a little time to process Nancy's death. Maybe she'll have remembered something that'll help." Cassie stepped out of the jeep and followed after Tessa. "So many beautiful decorations on these houses. But none on Marie's." She glanced around the neighborhood as Tessa knocked. "I wonder why."

"Her husband died a few years ago. Maybe she just can't do it on her own." Tessa smiled as the door swung open. "Hi, Marie. Sorry to bother you."

"Oh, it's all right. I don't mind a little company." Marie waved them inside. "Are you here to tell me that you know who killed Nancy?"

"Unfortunately, not quite yet." Tessa stepped inside. "But we hope to be able to tell you that very soon. Maybe with your help."

"I'll do anything I can to help, but I'm afraid I don't have much to say. I don't really know anything about Nancy's murder."

Cassie swept her gaze around the living room. She noticed many photographs hung on the walls and perched on tables throughout the space. As she looked at the faces in each of the pictures, she smiled at the different adventures Marie had taken part in.

"You ran in marathons?"

"Yes. And hiked mountains." Marie grinned as she picked up one of the pictures that featured her water-skiing. "My husband, Lloyd, used to say that he'd married a hot-air balloon." She laughed as she waved her hand. "I know that might sound a bit insulting, but that's not how he meant it. He said I traveled everywhere and rarely touched down. He was right. There was nothing I didn't want to try. When I wasn't out exploring, I was with Nancy." She pressed her hand to her chest as her voice wavered. "I still can't believe she's gone. We spent every spare minute we had together."

"I'm so sorry. You must miss her so much." Cassie looked into her eyes. "I'm sure you two shared all of your secrets."

"I thought we did." Marie set the picture back down. "Once. But things changed. I guess they always do. I'd break a hip if I tried to water-ski now. Now, it's just me and these ghosts of me." She laughed, then sighed. "I always pictured Nancy and me growing old together. Sitting on matching rocking chairs, watching sunsets, laughing about all the stupid things we did. Even after Lloyd died, I didn't feel alone, because I always had her." She smiled as she looked between Cassie and Tessa. "You two have that kind of friendship, too. I can tell."

"We do." Tessa smiled in return. "Which makes me even more determined to find out what happened to Nancy. Maybe it will give you some peace."

"I doubt it." Marie shook her head. "I heard that Devon has been arrested. I guess it makes sense that he'd be the killer. I tried to tell her it wasn't worth the risk that came with trying to catch him, but she was determined. I guess in the end, she tried a little too hard."

"Is this you and Sally?" Cassie smiled as she picked up a picture frame that contained an old photograph.

"It is." Marie looked at the picture. "We were in our teens there."

"What happened to Sally's arm? Did she break it?" Cassie showed the picture to Tessa, who peered over her shoulder.

"Oh yes. It was a terrible break. Of course, she blamed Nancy for it. Those two were always at each other's throats. We'd all been foolish, but only Sally got hurt. We took our bicycles to the steepest hill we could find, then rode down it with our feet perched up on the handlebars. It was stupid, of course, but back then it felt like a great adventure. Nancy lost control of her bike, and it bumped into Sally's. Sally veered off the road into some rocks and she went flying. She landed on her arm and broke it in three places." Marie ran her hand down her other arm. "I'll never forget that scream."

"I can understand why Sally screamed." Cassie stared at the picture.

"Oh no, Sally passed out right away. It was Nancy who screamed. She thought she'd really hurt her sister, or even worse, poor thing. No matter how much they fought, Nancy really did love her." Marie took the picture from Cassie and set it back down on the table. "I wish I could be of more help to you two, but I just don't know how I can be."

"Did you really not know about Nina?" Tessa looked straight at her. "You didn't suspect? Even when Nancy disappeared for all that time?"

"I didn't know." Marie narrowed her eyes. "Of course, I knew something was wrong for her to disappear like that. But she told me she'd gone off to care for a sick aunt. I knew that was a lie. I thought if she could lie to me like that, maybe we weren't as close as I thought we were. It hurt my feelings, actually, so I didn't ask her too many questions. Now, of course, I wish I had. She must have felt so lonely then."

"Thanks for your time, Marie." Tessa clasped her hands together. "I know it must be hard to talk about her."

"Very." Marie winced.

Tessa's phone rang. "Excuse me one second. Oh, it's Mirabel. Cassie, here." She handed the phone to Cassie.

"Hi, Mirabel?" Cassie turned away from them. "I've lost my phone. Is it there by any chance?

Maybe on the counter or under it?" She paused. "Are you sure?" She shook her head as Tessa looked at her.

"Just hang up and call it, then she might be able to spot it." Tessa glanced at Marie. "Sorry about this."

"It's no trouble, but I do have things to do." Marie gestured to the door. "I sure hope you find your phone, Cassie."

"Me, too." Cassie followed Tessa's instructions. She dialed her phone number on Tessa's phone as Marie led them to the door. As she heard the ringing on the phone, she also heard the sound of her ringtone. "What?" She pulled the phone away from her ear and listened just as Marie started to close the door. "That's my phone ringing!"

CHAPTER 21

Tessa held her hand against the door before Marie could close it. "Marie! Do you have Cassie's phone?"

"Cassie's phone? Why would I have it?" Marie shook her head and stepped back from the door.

"I can hear it ringing!" Cassie moved back into the house. "There! I think it's coming from your purse."

"Oh dear, you're right!" Marie gasped as she picked up her purse. "How is that possible?" She pulled Cassie's phone out of her purse and held it up. "Is this it?"

"Yes!" Cassie took it from her and smiled.

"But how did you end up with it?" Tessa studied Marie.

"I have no idea." Marie frowned, then snapped her fingers. "Oh, I stopped into the diner for a coffee and pie while you were working today. Remember, Cassie?"

"Yes, I remember."

"I must have picked it up thinking it was mine." Marie cringed. "I'm so sorry for the trouble I caused you. I just haven't been able to think straight since Nancy died."

"It's all right, Marie. I understand." Cassie started to turn away from the door, then paused. "Marie, do you have any idea why Nancy cut her sister out of her will?"

"Oh, she did it about once a month." Marie rolled her eyes. "Whenever the two fought, Nancy would declare that Sally was out of the will. She paid her lawyer a small fortune to keep changing it. I always thought it was foolish because she had so much life left to live. But I guess I was wrong." She sniffled as she closed the door.

Tessa led the way toward the jeep. "I guess that explains the change in the will."

"Yes, it was probably just bad timing for Sally. But if Sally knew that Nancy had just changed the will, why would she choose now to kill her sister?" Cassie settled in the passenger seat.

"I'm not sure. Maybe she didn't know. Maybe she just lost it. That was odd, wasn't it?" Tessa started the jeep. "Do you really think she picked up your phone by accident?"

"Why else would she pick it up? She had no reason to steal my phone. I did spend quite some time talking with her. I might have put my phone down right next to her without realizing it. Silly mistake, but at least it had a good outcome. I'm sure that as soon as she noticed she had it, she would have brought it back to me. But I did notice something else pretty strange." Cassie pulled her notebook out of her purse and jotted down a note. "In all of the pictures that Marie had around her house, I didn't see a single picture of Nancy."

"What about the one with Sally in it?" Tessa glanced over at her.

"No, it was just Marie and Sally." Cassie shook her head. "It just seems odd that she wouldn't have any photographs of Nancy around after they'd spent so much of their lives together."

"Maybe she took them down after Nancy died. It could be too hard for her to look at them. That might explain why I didn't see any pictures of her husband, either. It could be part of how she grieves." Tessa turned down the street that led toward their houses. "But the fact that Sally broke her arm the way she did, it does make me wonder if she would have even been able to wield the ax that killed Nancy. It's not a light tool. If she had injuries that would prevent her from being able to swing it, then we might be able to eliminate her as a suspect."

"But she went to the ax-throwing place with Nina, Marie, and Nancy, right? So she must have been able to throw one."

"Actually, I called to find out if any of the women had taken an ax with them, and the person I spoke to said that Nancy brought her own, and the rest used the ones there. And that Sally used a much lighter ax than the others. It was much smaller than the one that was used to kill Nancy, and lighter. So, it's possible that Sally could wield that, but not the one that killed Nancy. I think, given her injury and the fact that it seems she would have trouble handling a large ax, it makes her a much less likely suspect." Tessa turned onto their street, just as her phone started to ring. "Can you see who that is?"

"It's Mirabel."

"Go ahead, answer it."

"Hi, Mirabel, it's Cassie. We found my phone."

"That's great news, Cassie, but that's not what I called about. Apparently, Sally is at the tree farm creating quite a commotion. Ollie just took off from here with lights and sirens. Have you heard about it? Do you know what's happening there?"

"We haven't heard about it. But we're only a few minutes away. We'll head right over and see if we can find out anything." Cassie ended the call and looked over at Tessa. "Turn around. We need to go to Nancy's farm. Something sent Ollie running over there. Maybe if we go over, we can find out what it is."

"On it." Tessa whipped the jeep around, then stepped on the gas.

Cassie typed out a text to let Sebastian know she had found her phone. Once she sent it, she flipped to the main screen only to find that several of her apps were open.

"That's funny, I don't remember opening these." Cassie began closing them. "I don't usually have so many things open on my phone."

"Do you think Marie went through it?" Tessa turned down the road that led to Nancy's farm. "She says she picked it up by accident and didn't notice it, but maybe she's lying."

"Why would she go through it?" Cassie shook her head. "She'd have no reason to."

"Unless." Tessa pursed her lips.

"Unless what?"

"Unless she was worried that you were onto something, maybe the fact that she killed Nancy." Tessa turned down the street that led to the farm. "Why else would she have stolen your phone?"

"Well, we don't know that she stole it." Cassie stared down at the screen. "It's possible I left the apps open and just didn't realize it. I'm probably just being paranoid."

"Or not paranoid enough."

"What do you mean?" Cassie glanced at her.

"You can be a little too trusting, Cassie." Tessa turned down the driveway of the farm.

"I don't know if I'd say I'm too trusting." Cassie shifted in her seat. "But you certainly aren't trusting enough."

"Excuse me?"

"You're always suspicious of people." Cassie shrugged. "It's in your nature and developed from years of working for the police. Sometimes people aren't always up to no good. Sometimes they just genuinely want to be part of your life. Marie was Nancy's best friend. She had no real motive to kill her. Why would she decide to kill her? She had no reason to take my phone. It was just an honest mistake."

"If you say so." Tessa parked and pulled open the door. "I just want to get this murder solved."

Cassie started doubting herself. Was she too trusting? Did Marie really steal her phone? Her thoughts were swept away by the sound of angry shouting farther up the driveway.

CHAPTER 22

Cassie focused on the shouting match between Nina and Sally. "It looks like this is about to get out of control." She hoped Oliver wouldn't be long.

"What's going on?" Tessa marched straight toward the two women. "Break it up, you two!"

"She needs to leave my property!" Nina shouted straight at Sally. "I've asked her nicely, I've asked her not so nicely, and now I'm ready to throw her off myself, if she doesn't leave."

"Don't you even think about touching me!" Sally inched closer to Nina. "I'm not going anywhere! I've spent more than half of my life on this property. My sister worked her fingers to the bone to make it a success, and I will not allow you to destroy it."

"I'm not destroying it. She left it to me, Sally! Sorry if that hurts you, but that's what happened! It's mine, and you're the one that's trespassing!" Nina scowled. "I've called the police! I'm going to get you removed from my property! You're causing a disturbance!"

"You're the one that should be arrested! I knew it! I knew it!" Sally glared at Nina. "I knew you were selling all of my sister's things!"

"I just needed space for the memorial!" Nina snapped.

"Save it." Sally waved a receipt through the air. "I know you just sold the couch to a friend of mine. We have the whole thing recorded! You're not going to con your way out of it this time."

"Let's try to calm down." Tessa stepped between them.

"She stole the couch and sold it." Sally held the receipt toward Tessa's face.

"I didn't steal anything. I own these things." Nina looked at Tessa. "I'm going to inherit the contents of the house, which means I can do whatever I want with them."

"Not yet. The estate hasn't been finalized, yet." Tessa looked over at Nina. "You don't legally own them."

"She lied to me," Sally sputtered as she glared at Nina. "She said all the items were going into storage, not being sold!"

"Nina, that's what you told us, too." Cassie narrowed her eyes. "Why did you lie about it?"

"I don't have to explain myself. These are going to be my things. I can do whatever I want with them." Nina spun on her heel and marched toward the house.

"This is how much my sister meant to you?" Sally shouted after her. "She's barely dead, and you're picking her house clean of anything of value? I knew it! I knew you didn't care about her at all!"

Nina slammed the front door shut.

"Sally, I know it's hard, but you have to let this go," Tessa said. "Nina's living on the property. If she wants to, she can probably press trespassing charges against you."

"Unbelievable!" Sally stared at the house. "It was my sister's. It was everything she worked for. It holds so many memories. Now, it's just gone? How could she do this to me!"

"Nina is grieving, too." Cassie stepped up beside Sally. "This just might be her way of handling it. She's probably not doing it to you on purpose."

"I'm not talking about her." Sally gasped. "I'm

talking about my sister! I just don't understand why she would leave everything she built to a woman she barely knew!"

"Her daughter." Tessa cleared her throat. "You're forgetting that part."

"No, I'm not." Sally crossed her arms. "I don't care what anyone says, that woman is not my sister's child. There's not a trace of Nancy in her! The more I get to know her, the more convinced I am of that."

"All that matters is that Nancy loved her." Tessa lowered her voice. "She wanted to make sure she was taken care of, and that she would have what she needed for the future. Sally, I'm sorry that you're going through this, and this happened to your sister, but you have to consider what your sister would have wanted."

"Do I?" Sally glared at her. "Why do I have to consider anything that my sister wanted? She obviously didn't care about me!"

"She loved you, Sally." Tessa stepped closer to her. "It might not all make sense right now, but I have no doubt that she loved you."

"Sure, whatever you say." Sally looked at the driveway as Oliver's car pulled up.

"What's going on here, Sally?" Oliver walked up to her.

"Why should I bother telling you. You won't do anything about it. I'm leaving." Sally shook her head as she walked back down the driveway.

"Are you going to just let her go?" Cassie watched Sally leave as Tessa explained what they had just witnessed.

"With that kind of anger, I'd say she might have been able to kill her sister," Tessa said.

"Maybe, but I can't hold her." Oliver looked between them. "I had to release Devon. Make sure you stay out of his way."

"You released him?" Tessa raised her eyebrows.

"I had to, at least for the moment. I don't have any proof to link him to the murder. There are no fingerprints on the ax, and any DNA that might be on it is going to take a few days to come back." Oliver crossed his arms. "He also has an alibi. He claims that he was with his girlfriend at the time of the murder, and she insists that he was. I have no reason to hold him at the moment."

"But he was about to take off!" Cassie's voice grew stern. "Doesn't that mean anything?"

"Unfortunately, not really. He's free to leave the area. We don't really know if he was going to take off. He claims he wasn't." Oliver crossed his arms. "But he has agreed to stay in town. He's insisting that he wants to find out who the killer is. And he also repeated the same allegations that Nina is not who she says she is."

"Mark is having a hard time verifying her identity. He thinks that she might have been part of an illegal adoption. If that's the case, then it would explain why it's hard to identify her," Tessa said.

"Hopefully, I'll get some useful answers soon. I'm going to speak to Nina." Oliver started toward the house, then glanced over his shoulder. "I'll see you at the parade tomorrow?"

"We'll be there." Tessa started back toward the jeep.

"I can't believe Devon's on the loose again." Cassie followed after Tessa.

"His alibi is paper-thin. I'm sure his girlfriend would say anything to protect him." Tessa walked beside her. "Him being on the loose is only going to make things more complicated."

"I know." Cassie glanced over at her. "But maybe he's telling the truth."

"I doubt that man has ever told the truth," Tessa muttered. "But I guess with his record and his attitude, it's easy to assume he's lying. But think about it. Nina shows up out of the blue, her mother is murdered, and now she's inheriting everything?

She's also selling all of her possessions very quickly? It seems pretty suspicious to me."

"I hear you." Cassie slid into the passenger seat. "It seems that every time I'm convinced I know who it is, everything changes. Sally was a great suspect, but now that we know it's very unlikely she could swing the ax, she's probably innocent. I'm not going to eliminate her entirely, but I think we should focus elsewhere first. So, where do we go from here?"

"Sally made a good point." Tessa started the jeep. "Even if she and Nancy weren't as close as they could have been, they were still sisters. They still grew up together. If Sally says Nina is nothing like her sister, then maybe she's right."

"Maybe. But remember, Nina wasn't raised by Nancy. Who knows what her childhood was like. It's not too surprising that they wouldn't have a lot in common. But Devon claims that Nina isn't who she says she is. Do you think he might be right? What if Nina really is lying about who she is? This whole thing could be a con. If Nancy found out about it, maybe things got out of control."

"If she's lying about who she is, she has to know that the lawyer will figure it out eventually." Tessa tapped her fingertips against the steering wheel. "Maybe she thought her best chance of getting something from Nancy was to act quickly and kill her before the truth came out. If that's the case, she does have a good motive to kill her mother. Unfortunately, it looks like that is going to take some time to prove. We still have Kevin to consider, and Devon is certainly not off the hook."

"I think we should focus on Kevin. If we can't prove that Nina did it, at the moment, and Devon apparently has an alibi, that leaves us Kevin. We know that he has a yellow bird, which would explain the yellow feather on Nancy's coat sleeve. He doesn't have any alibi, and he has a pretty decent motive."

"Well, maybe he'll be at the parade tomorrow. He said he was hoping to go. No kid in town is going to miss it." Tessa pulled into her driveway.

"I have the morning shift at the diner, then I'll come over, so we can pack everything up and head to the parade?" Cassie opened the door to the jeep.

"Great." Tessa smiled.

The following morning, after finishing her shift at the diner, Cassie went straight to Tessa's house. She helped her round up the goats and secure them in the back of the jeep. As she did, she ran through all of the clues they had discovered so far. None of them pointed in one solid direction, at least not that she could see.

"Let's go, Harry!" Tessa clapped her hands together as she called the dog.

Harry bounded around the side of the house and hopped into the jeep alongside the goats.

"Are those elf ears?" Cassie giggled at the sight of the headband perched on Harry's head.

"Yes." Tessa grinned as she started the jeep. "I

thought for sure he'd chew them to bits, but he seems to like them."

"Adorable." Cassie grinned as she petted the dog.

"He does have a special talent for bringing a smile to everyone's face." Tessa pulled out into the street. "It looks like the snow is going to hold off for a while."

Cassie glanced at her phone as she received a text. "Sebastian is going to meet us at the park for the parade. Is Mark really going to be part of it?"

"I think so." Tessa grinned as she turned down the street that led to the large park in the center of town. "He was Santa at the fair last year, and he was wearing that suit all day yesterday."

"And wearing it well." Cassie laughed.

"Wow, the parking lot is already crowded." Tessa turned into the park and found a spot not too far from the entrance. "The pen should already be set up for the goats. We just have to get them in it." She grabbed their leashes.

"I'll get the cookies." Cassie gathered the containers of cookies and the trays to put them on.

Harry led the way through the crowd. His elf ears drew lots of attention.

"Look at him loving on everyone." Cassie

laughed. "This might be one of the best days of his life."

"It is. Look at all the treats people are giving him." Tessa shook her head. "He's not going to need to eat for a week. I think he paired up with the goats to steal that bowl of frosting yesterday. I still haven't figured out how he managed it."

"Oh no, if they've started working together, it's all over." Cassie laughed as she opened the gate on the pen.

The goats bolted inside and began exploring the area. Harry followed in after them.

"Oh, do you want to spend some time together? Play nice. I'll come check on you after the parade." Tessa closed the gate and set the latch. "With these three, you can never be too careful. If they get the chance, they'll devour all of the cookies before anyone else has a chance to. The petting zoo and snacks don't start until after the parade, so we have a few minutes to look for Kevin."

"Good." Cassie glanced around at the crowd. "Sebastian and Stephanie should be here soon."

"Harry, stay here and guard the goats." Tessa patted the top of Harry's head. She squinted toward the parade. "I can't see Mark. There's a large crowd watching the parade. How are we going to find Kevin in all of this?"

"If he's even here." Cassie searched the faces that passed her by.

"If he's here, I'm sure he's with his kids. So, where would kids want to be at an event like this?" Tessa peered into a crowd near a hot-chocolate cart. "I think that might be him over there."

Cassie caught sight of Kevin, with two children beside him. A boy, who looked to be about ten, and a girl, a few years younger.

"Now is our chance to talk to him." Cassie took a deep breath.

"It is. Let's see what he has to say." Tessa walked toward the cart.

Kevin took two cups of hot chocolate from the vendor. "These aren't meant to be too hot, kids, but you still have to be careful." He held them out to them.

"Daddy, are you going to bring us a treat at our house, like before?" The little girl grinned up at him. "We've kept it a secret, like you said!"

"A secret, huh?" Tessa stepped up beside them. "Are you two good at keeping secrets?"

Kevin looked from Tessa to Cassie, then back to his children.

"We didn't tell Mom at all!" The young boy smiled. "She would have been so mad if she knew we had ice cream before lunch."

"It has to stay a secret." Kevin cleared his throat, then glanced up at Cassie and Tessa. "I surprised them with some ice cream while they were with their sitter. It's no big deal."

"When was this?" Tessa asked.

"Last week." Kevin waved his hand through the air.

"It was two days ago, Daddy!" The little girl jumped up and down. "You said you would do it again next week, and I've been counting the days!"

"Wait a minute." Cassie crouched down in front of the child. "Was this in the morning?"

"Yes, a bit before lunch!"

"Carli, quiet!" Kevin looked down at his daughter. "It's a secret, remember?"

"A secret?" Tessa stared at him.

"Go play that game over there, okay? Give me a minute to talk with these ladies." Kevin handed his children a few dollars.

"Okay!" The young boy took his sister's hand and led the way.

Tessa watched the kids walk away, then looked back at Kevin.

"Why would you want to keep it a secret? It sounds like your alibi. If you were with your kids and the sitter, then you obviously weren't at the farm with Nancy."

"Please, you can't tell anyone." Kevin kept his gaze on his children as he spoke. "I wasn't supposed to see them. My ex is being really hard on me about when I can visit them because I haven't been able to provide child support this month. If she finds out that I was with them when I wasn't supposed to be, she'll have me right back in court, and fire the sitter. She's a sweet kid. I don't want her getting in trouble because of me."

"You were willing to go to jail to keep the peace with your ex?" Tessa asked incredulously. "Have you lost your mind?"

"No." Kevin's voice hardened. "I'll do whatever it takes to make sure that I'm in their lives. I know I didn't kill Nancy, and I know there would be no evidence to prove that I did. So, why should I have to blow up any chance I have of being with my kids just because I happened to know someone who was killed? Please, don't ruin this. This is my day with them. I just want them to have the best holiday they can."

"Of course." Cassie smiled as she looked down

you do something so terrible to a woman who only showed you kindness?"

"I didn't kill her!" Nina scowled.

"No? Well, that's hard for me to believe after you lied about being her long-lost daughter and conned her into leaving you everything in her will!" Tessa crossed her arms.

"All right, fine! I might have done that." Nina sniffled.

"Might have?" Tessa glared at her. "We just heard your confession!"

"Yes, yes, I did! But I didn't kill her! I'm friends with her real daughter. When she told me she knew who her mother was but had no interest in meeting her, I saw an opportunity. So, I used her details and I came here. The plan was to just take whatever I could from her." Nina wrung her hands together. "I thought it would be an easy job, with a solid payout. I never expected that she would actually leave me everything, and I never expected that someone would kill her."

"But when she found out you were lying, she threatened to have you arrested, right? So, you had to kill her!" Cassie said.

"No! No, I didn't kill her! I wouldn't have! Even if she had found out the truth, I wouldn't have. You're right. She was so kind to me. I never really had a family, especially not a mother, and the way she took me in right away, it surprised me. She wanted to make sure I had everything I needed. I've never been taken care of like that before. I started out wanting to take what I could, but honestly, in the end, I just wanted to keep being her daughter. I had hoped she would never find out, and maybe we could just be a family. She didn't know I wasn't her daughter, so what harm could it do?"

"Sure, it seemed like you really cared about her when you started selling all of her things!" Tessa shook her head. "You're a true con artist, Nina, and you're not getting away with murder."

"I didn't kill her! I had no choice but to sell her things. These guys from my past showed up. They knew about the scheme, and they said if I didn't pay them off, they would tell everyone the truth. I knew that if they did, I would go to prison. I knew no one would believe me if they found out." Nina sobbed as Oliver began to jog toward them. "Please, don't let him put me in prison for something I didn't do! I didn't kill her!"

"You're right. No one is going to believe you." Tessa looked at Oliver as he reached them. "Ollie, we just caught Nina here admitting that she's not Nina."

"I know you're not Nancy's daughter." Oliver looked at Nina. "We finally got confirmation on your true identity. Heather, isn't it? You're not in any way related to Nancy. You've been on the wrong side of the law your whole life. Now, I know you had every reason to kill her."

"But I didn't! I loved her!" Nina tried to break free of his grasp.

Oliver swung her arm behind her back and closed a handcuff around it. "You're under arrest for murder."

"You can throw me in prison, but you won't be putting the right person away!" Nina sobbed as he closed the other handcuff around her wrist. "Nancy was a good person! She deserves to have her real killer caught!"

"Let's go." Oliver led Nina back toward his car.

CHAPTER 24

Cassie watched as the snow began falling, and the crowd continued to celebrate. Most were unaware that a murderer had just been whisked away.

"Do you think she really meant it? Do you think she actually cared about Nancy?"

"How could she? She killed her. She took a woman who had a good heart, stole from her, conned her into believing her daughter had come home to her, and then killed her to cover it up. It's the only thing that makes sense. I don't care what she says. She's a criminal. That doesn't change because someone shows you a little bit of love and attention."

"I guess not." Cassie shrugged. "It certainly does make sense. She had every reason to kill Nancy. She was worried the truth was going to come out eventually, especially with those two men threatening to tell the truth. Maybe Nina, or Heather, I guess, thought if Nancy was dead, she would have more chance of being able to get hold of her stuff and sell it off before the truth was revealed."

"Sally and Devon were right. They tried to tell us that Nina wasn't who she claimed to be."

"She's a good liar. A very good liar." Cassie crossed her arms. "And to think I was ready to see Kevin arrested and pulled away from his children. My instincts must be really off. I honestly still feel bad for Nina, I mean, Heather. She must have had a very hard life, if she became cold enough to murder someone who treated her so well."

"Maybe. Or maybe she was just born wrong. Some people don't have the capacity for empathy." Tessa looked toward a woman walking away from the crowd. "There's Marie. We should let her know that an arrest has been made. It might give her some small comfort."

"That's true." Cassie walked toward her. "It looks like she's headed for the Christmas tree in the center of the park. She must not feel up to watching the parade."

"Let's catch up to her. Maybe she'll feel differently when we tell her the good news." Tessa quickened her pace.

As the rest of the crowd headed for the main walkway of the park, Cassie caught up to Marie near the large Christmas tree.

"Marie!" Cassie waved her hand through the air.

Marie continued to walk as if she hadn't heard Cassie.

"Marie!" Tessa jogged up to her. Despite the slight limp in her gait, she was still quite fast. "Stop! We need to talk to you!"

Marie walked faster.

"Marie!" Tessa broke into a run and managed to catch up to her. "Just stop!"

"No!" Marie swung around to face Tessa, and in one swift movement she pulled Tessa back against her chest. "You won't take me! Never!"

"Marie!" Cassie gasped at the sight of the knife she gripped in her hand. "Let Tessa go! Don't hurt her!"

"I won't let her go!" Marie placed the knife against Tessa's stomach. "Don't move! Don't even think about yelling for help!"

"Just put down the knife, Marie." Cassie stared into her eyes as she tried to ignore the panic welling up inside of her. "This doesn't have to end this way. We can help you figure all of this out."

"Help me figure what out?" Marie kept the knife pressed against Tessa's stomach as she stared back at Cassie. "There's nothing to figure out. I did exactly what needed to be done." She smirked as she shook her head. "When Nina first showed up, I was shocked. I thought there was no way it could be true. My best friend, a woman I considered to be a sister for the majority of my life, never would have kept this kind of secret from me for so long. She would have told me right away. She would have known that I would help her." She winced as Tessa jerked to the side. "Stop it, now, or I'm going to make sure that it takes longer than it needs to. Understand?" She tightened her grip on her.

Tessa narrowed her eyes but remained still.

"So what if she didn't tell you about the pregnancy?" Cassie's heart pounded. "Why was that enough to kill her? Some people have secrets they can't share with anyone."

"Only because they have a reason to be ashamed." Marie's lips tightened. "At first I was so hurt. I was sure that I must have been a terrible friend, that we weren't as close as I imagined we were. Why else would she hide it from me?"

"But then you realized why." Tessa kept her voice low as she spoke. "She had to hide it from you."

"But why?" Cassie glanced around the surrounding area. There was no one around. Everyone was watching the parade. "Why would she need to hide it from you?"

"Because of who the father was, right?" Tessa's jaw tensed. "Because there was no way that Nancy could tell you the truth about the baby."

"Exactly. Well done. We met in grade school, you know. My husband and I." Marie smiled. "It was love at first sight, before we were supposed to be able to love. We followed each other all through high school, and then college. We had known each other for so long, he didn't even propose to me, he didn't have to. We just started planning our wedding. We always knew we would be together, just like I always knew that Nancy would be my maid of honor. And she was. She helped me plan everything, and she made a lovely toast at our wedding." She squeezed her eyes shut for a moment. "It was so perfect, thanks to her. She was the best person in my life."

"And that best person made a terrible mistake, didn't she?" Tessa whispered.

Cassie's heart dropped as she began to piece together the scenario. All at once she knew how much danger Tessa was really in. Marie had nothing to lose, and she imagined she would do anything to keep from going to jail.

"Your husband?" Cassie took a sharp breath. "He was the father of Nancy's baby?"

CHAPTER 25

Cassie's mind whirled with the realization that Marie's husband was Nina's father.

"How did you figure it out?" Tessa asked Marie.

"I suspected something once. I was away visiting my parents for a few days, not long after we got married. I had to miss a party for a friend while I was away, but when Lloyd picked me up from the airport, I found a feather from Nancy's dress in the car. I had helped her pick it out at the store for the party. It had yellow feathers all over it. It looked so gorgeous on her." Marie's voice cracked. "I kept that feather all this time. When I asked him about it, he was so cagey. He said it must have been there from before, when she was in the car with me. But I was never in his car with her after she had bought the dress. Then he said, oh she had borrowed his car to get home from the party. I knew she would never drive, even if she had one drink. It just didn't add up. I thought it was odd, but Nancy told me the same story." She tightened the grip on the knife. "So, I believed them. I guess I didn't want to face the truth."

"But then Nina showed up," Tessa said.

"Yes, it wasn't until Nina showed up, and I did the math as to when Nancy would have been pregnant, that I added it all up." Tears slipped down Marie's cheeks. "It's funny. I had an entire marriage with my husband, a relationship that lasted practically his entire lifetime, and not once did I doubt his love or loyalty. But years after Lloyd died, I discovered how deeply he had betrayed me. But it wasn't his betrayal that broke my heart. It was hers. Not just because she'd had an affair with him and had his baby, but because she'd hidden it from me, such an important part of her life, as if I didn't matter at all." She shook her head. "Can you imagine that? She told Sally, who she could barely stand, instead of me. She told Sally everything."

"It sounds to me like she might have wanted to protect you." Cassie took a small step forward as her hands itched with the urge to pry the knife away from her. "And she did in a way. You got to enjoy your marriage with your husband."

"My lie? Yes, I got to enjoy my lie. They made a fool out of me! When I confronted her about it, she didn't even shout, or try to deny it. She started to cry, as if she had a reason to be hurt. She said that she never wanted to hurt me, that she had been drunk, and he offered to give her a lift home, and it just happened. That my husband loved me. She loved me. And they regretted it as soon as it happened. When she found out she was pregnant, she thought about telling me, but he insisted that she didn't. So she disappeared instead." Marie rolled her eyes. "As if that didn't break my heart on its own. She spent decades lying to me, letting me believe that my husband loved me. She was a terrible friend, and the whole time I wondered if I was the one that had done something wrong to make her disappear the way she did. For all those months."

Cassie's heart pounded. With everyone watching the parade, she knew that they wouldn't be missed. Oliver thought he already had the killer in custody, and he wouldn't think twice about them possibly being in danger. Sebastian and Stephanie would be too busy with the parade to even consider that they might need help. Her stomach churned as she realized that she and Tessa were alone. Her muscles ached with the urge to lunge at Marie, but the way she had the knife positioned made her certain that Tessa would get hurt or even killed in the process.

"Please, Marie." Cassie held up her hands. "I don't want anyone to get hurt here. Just let go of Tessa. Just let her go, and you can take off into the woods. Ollie already arrested Nina. We found out she was lying about who she is. She's going to go to prison for killing Nancy. You don't have to worry. All you have to do is let Tessa go."

"Let her go?" Marie laughed. "Not a chance. People can't be trusted."

"I'm so sorry that you were hurt the way you were, Marie." Cassie inched a little closer to her. "But Nancy did that to you, not Tessa. Not everyone will betray you."

"Yes, they will! The man I loved for most of my life, and the best friend I loved for most of my life, betrayed me, and lied to me for decades!" Marie let out a wail as she tightened her grasp on Tessa. "I won't go to prison for her! Or for him! I won't go to prison when they are the ones that did something wrong!"

"Marie, please!" Cassie let out a shriek as she

saw Marie's hand that held the knife tighten and jerk toward Tessa.

Just then, a loud creak cut through her scream. An instant later, the entire Christmas tree toppled forward and struck Marie and Tessa from behind. The two disappeared inside the large branches of the tree.

A smattering of barking followed by a yelp echoed through the air.

"Tessa!" Cassie screamed as she lunged toward the tree.

Before she could reach it, a flash of red brushed past her and dove right into the branches.

Cassie dug through the tree limbs in an attempt to find Tessa. Her hand brushed across something cold and hard. She flinched as she realized it had to be the knife. She carefully wrapped her hand around it and tugged.

Cassie pulled the knife from the branches and screamed at the sight of blood splattered across its silver blade.

"Tessa!"

"I've got her! I've got her, Cassie!" Mark's muffled voice reached her from beyond the branches of the Christmas tree. He emerged from the wreckage of ribbons, ornaments, and Christmas lights, with Tessa wrapped up in his arms.

Cassie caught sight of a smear of blood on Tessa's shirt, right before she heard the rustle of the branches on the other side of the tree.

Marie burst out from under the tree and lunged toward the woods.

"No, you don't!" Cassie shouted and launched herself toward the fleeing woman. She felt her body collide with Marie's and wrapped her arms around her shoulders and chest as they both fell to the ground.

CHAPTER 26

Cassie pinned Marie down to the ground beneath her.

"Is Tessa alive? Tell me!" Cassie looked up from the writhing woman on the ground and straight at Mark.

"Yes, Cassie, she's alive." Mark continued to hold Tessa in his arms. "She's knocked out, though. Something on the tree must have hit her."

"But I saw blood! Did she get stabbed? Look her over!" Cassie tightened her grip as Marie tried to slip out from under her.

"No, it's not her blood, Cassie. I've checked." Mark shouted toward someone who ran in their direction. "Hurry! We're going to need an ambulance!"

Cassie's mind swirled as she recognized it was Sebastian running toward them. He pulled his phone out of his pocket. She looked at the woman she still held beneath her. Suddenly, she saw the bloodstain spreading across Marie's white blouse.

"Marie?" Cassie stared down at her. She looked her over and realized Marie had just cut her hand.

"Cassie, are you okay?" Sebastian ran up behind her, out of breath, with the phone pressed to his ear.

"Yes, but Marie must have cut her hand when the tree crashed down." Cassie looked at her. "She'll be fine. Tessa is still knocked out."

"Put me down!" Tessa's shrill voice broke through Cassie's explanation.

"Nope, she's awake." Mark shifted her in his arms but did not put her down. "Tessa, listen to me."

"Mark!" Tessa squirmed in his grasp. "Put me down, now!"

"No!" Mark stared hard into her eyes. "I won't until you listen to me!"

"What happened?" Tessa stared at Cassie. "Are you okay, Cassie?"

"I'm okay, Tessa, just really glad to hear your voice." Cassie shifted to the side as Sebastian crouched down beside her and placed his hands on Marie's shoulders to keep her still.

"Tessa, I'll put you down, but you have to promise me that you will sit down and stay sitting down. You were hit pretty hard on the head when the tree fell. You could have a concussion. Okay?" Mark's gaze bored into hers.

"Hit on the head?" Tessa stared back at him, then blinked. After a moment, she rested her head against his chest and closed her eyes. "This is fine, actually. I think I'll just take a little rest."

"No, no, Tessa." Mark placed a light kiss on her cheek. "You have to stay awake."

"Mark!" Tessa huffed. "What are you doing kissing me?"

"I have to keep you awake somehow." Mark grinned. "Are you still feeling sleepy?" He puckered his lips.

"Don't you dare!" Tessa scowled at him. "I'm wide awake."

"Good." Mark tipped his head toward a crew of paramedics that ran toward them. "Then you'll be ready to get checked out." He eased her down gently as the paramedics reached them. "She was out for at least a few minutes. I'm not sure what hit her, but probably a branch of the tree."

As Tessa argued with the paramedic, another set

and two officers ran over to Marie. Cassie stepped back and looked over at Tessa with tears in her eyes.

"It's all right." Sebastian pulled her into his arms. "Everything's all right now. Tessa is going to be just fine."

"Once these people stop poking and prodding me!" Tessa swatted at the paramedics.

Mark caught her hands and held them tight. "You're going to do everything they say. Understand? I did not pull you out from under that tree just to have you be too stubborn to get treated. You took a heavy blow, and I'm going to make sure that you're okay."

"It would be best if we could take her to the hospital to monitor her." One of the paramedics smiled at Tessa. "Do you think you can come easily, or am I going to have to let your boyfriend here carry you to the ambulance?"

"He's not my boyfriend," Tessa huffed. "I'm not going anywhere, until I find out what exactly happened here. The last thing I remember was Marie grabbing me."

"I was so scared, Tessa." Cassie walked up beside her and took her hand. "I thought she'd killed you. When the tree fell, I was sure she'd stabbed you. Then Mark came running and pulled you right out from under the tree."

"But how did you know we needed help?" Tessa shifted her gaze to Mark.

"I didn't. I saw Harry messing with the latch on the goat pen. I tried to get to him before he could get it open, but he was too quick. Then the goats bolted, and he took off after them. I chased him to try to catch him because I knew how upset you would be. I spotted the goats gnawing on the Christmas tree. Then I saw that horrible woman holding you hostage. I tried to get to you, but the goats knocked down the tree before I could." Mark paused for a moment, then smiled. "Really, you have the goats to thank, and Harry."

"Don't worry, I've got them." Sebastian wrangled the two goats away from the tree as Harry circled them and barked.

"I guess their wild behavior isn't so bad after all." Tessa smiled. "I can't believe Marie almost got away with this."

"She wouldn't have." Oliver walked up to them as the ambulance carrying Marie drove away. "After I arrested Nina, I looked over the evidence again. I realized that the part shoe print in the snow had a pattern that matched a pair of Marie's husband's old boots that I'd seen at her house. They were wet, probably from the snow. My guess was, and she just admitted, that she put them on when she decided to kill Nancy, so that it would look like a man had killed her. But the boots were too big, and she walked on the tips of her toes to keep them from sliding off. That's why the whole print wasn't there. There were also a couple of tiny drops of blood on the boots, and I found a balled-up shirt she must have used when she killed Nancy, in the bottom of her trash can."

"But how did she get them off Nancy's farm without anyone noticing?" Cassie asked.

"She managed to clean up on the neighboring farm and dumped the boots and clothes by the creek there. She picked them up that night after the police left the area. She knows this area very well, from spending so much time with Nancy," Oliver explained.

"Marie planned to kill her." Tessa shook her head. "She didn't just snap. She must have spoken to Nancy about Nina being Lloyd's daughter, then came back to kill her."

"Yes, she definitely planned this. She just admitted to me that after she spoke to Nancy about Lloyd being the father, she went away and planned how to get rid of her, then arranged to meet her by the house, when everyone was on the other side of the farm involved in the hunt. She figured no one would be close enough to catch her, and she would have time to clean up, and with so many people around, there would be lots of possible suspects. But Nancy changed the meeting place and insisted she meet her at the wreath because she wanted to be close to the hunt. Marie agreed to meet her there. No one was close by at the time, so she followed through with her plan. I had just found the evidence and left Marie's house, when I heard the call for help come over the radio." Oliver looked at Cassie and Tessa. "At least you're both okay."

"We are." Tessa smiled. "I have to say, I had no idea it was actually Marie until she pulled out the knife. Then everything began to make sense. I'll write out everything she confessed to us."

"After you go to the hospital." Mark squeezed her hand. "Right?"

"Right." Tessa held his gaze. "Maybe I have the goats to thank for saving my life, Mark, but you were here right when I needed you. I won't forget that."

"No, I'm sure you won't, because I don't intend

to leave your side until you get a clean bill of health. And maybe a little longer." Mark smiled.

"We'll see." Tessa smiled in return.

Cassie took one of the goats from Sebastian. She leaned close to him and whispered, "How many times do you think she'll have to be hit on the head before she kisses him back?"

"Hopefully, not too many." Sebastian draped his arm around her shoulders. "But I'm familiar with stubborn streaks."

"Oh?" Cassie's eyes widened as she looked at him.

"Very familiar." Sebastian kissed her, then leaned back and looked into her eyes. "I think we'd better get these goats some cookies. They deserve lots of treats."

"Yes, and Harry, too." Cassie reached down to pet the dog who had stretched out beside her legs.

He watched as Tessa climbed into the ambulance.

Mark climbed in behind her.

Cassie crouched down beside Harry and kissed the top of his head.

"Don't worry, boy, she's in good hands."

As the snow continued to fall, the ambulance pulled away. A serenade of sirens filled the air. A voice over the PA system announced the end of the parade, and the start of the rest of the festivities. Warmth spread through Cassie despite the fear she'd felt just minutes before. With Nancy's killer on her way to prison, the town could celebrate Christmas.

The End

TESSA'S SUGAR COOKIE RECIPE

Ingredients:

Cookies:

3/4 cup butter, at room temperature

3/4 cup granulated sugar

1 egg, at room temperature

1 teaspoon vanilla extract

2 1/2 cups all-purpose flour

3/4 teaspoon baking powder

1/4 teaspoon salt

Frosting:

2 sticks (1 cup) butter

4 cups confectioners' sugar, sifted
2 tablespoons milk
1 teaspoon vanilla extract
Gel food coloring, optional

Preparation:

For the cookies:

Beat the butter in an electric mixer for 2 minutes. Add the sugar and beat together until light and fluffy.

Beat in the egg and vanilla extract.

Whisk together the flour, baking powder and salt in another bowl.

Gradually add the dry ingredients to the wet ingredients and mix until just combined. Don't overmix.

Form the dough into a ball. Divide into two and flatten into disks. Wrap in plastic wrap and refrigerate for at least 2 hours until firm.

When you are ready to bake the cookies, preheat the oven to 350 degrees Fahrenheit. Line two baking sheets with parchment paper.

Roll the dough on a lightly floured surface with a lightly floured rolling pin until about 1/4 inch thick. If the dough is too hard to roll when you take it out of the fridge, leave it for about 5 to 10 minutes at room temperature.

Using Christmas-themed cookie cutters, cut out the cookies and place on the baking sheets. Re-roll the leftover dough. If the dough gets too warm and sticky, return to the refrigerator to cool.

Bake for about 8 to 10 minutes until set and slightly browned around the edges. The baking time will vary depending on the size of the cookies.

Cool on the baking sheets for about 5 minutes, then transfer to a wire rack to cool completely.

For the buttercream frosting:

In a large bowl beat the butter until creamy. Gradually add the sifted confectioners' sugar and mix until well combined. Mix in the milk and vanilla extract.

If using food coloring, divide the frosting and add in the coloring, then mix until combined.

Decorate the cookies and leave them aside to set. The frosting won't set hard, but it will form a crust.

Enjoy!!

ABOUT THE AUTHOR

Cindy Bell is a USA Today and Wall Street Journal Bestselling Author. She is the author of over one hundred books in twelve series. Her cozies are set in small towns, with lovable animals, quirky characters, delicious food and a touch of romance. She loves writing twisty cozy mysteries that keep readers guessing until the end.

When she is not reading or writing, she loves baking (and eating) sweet treats or walking along the beach with Rufus, her energetic Cocker Spaniel, thinking of the next adventure her characters can embark on.

You can find out more about Cindy's books at www.cindybellbooks.com.

Cracked in Little Leaf Creek

Stung in Little Leaf Creek

Scandal In Little Leaf Creek

Dead in Little Leaf Creek

Scared in Little Leaf Creek

Felled in Little Leaf Creek

Deceit in Little Leaf Creek

MADDIE MILLS COZY MYSTERIES

Slain at the Sea

Homicide at the Harbor

Corpse at the Christmas Cookie Exchange

CHOCOLATE CENTERED COZY MYSTERIES

Chocolate Centered Cozy Mystery Series Box Set
(Books 1 - 4)

Chocolate Centered Cozy Mystery Series Box Set
(Books 5 - 8)

Chocolate Centered Cozy Mystery Series Box Set
(Books 9 - 12)

Chocolate Centered Cozy Mystery Series Box Set
(Books 13 - 16)

SAGE GARDENS COZY MYSTERIES

DUNE HOUSE COZY MYSTERIES

<u>Dune House Cozy Mystery Series 10 Book Box Set (Books 1 - 10)</u>

<u>Dune House Cozy Mystery Series Boxed Set 1 (Books 1 - 4)</u>

<u>Dune House Cozy Mystery Series Boxed Set 2 (Books 5 - 8)</u>

<u>Dune House Cozy Mystery Series Boxed Set 3 (Books 9 - 12)</u>

<u>Dune House Cozy Mystery Series Boxed Set 4 (Books 13 - 16)</u>

<u>Seaside Secrets</u>

<u>Boats and Bad Guys</u>

<u>Treasured History</u>

<u>Hidden Hideaways</u>

<u>Dodgy Dealings</u>

<u>Suspects and Surprises</u>

<u>Ruffled Feathers</u>

<u>A Fishy Discovery</u>

<u>Danger in the Depths</u>

<u>Celebrities and Chaos</u>

<u>Pups, Pilots and Peril</u>

WAGGING TAIL COZY MYSTERIES

Murder at Poodle Place

Murder at Hound Hill

Murder at Rover Meadows

Murder at the Pet Expo

Murder on Woof Way

NUTS ABOUT NUTS COZY MYSTERIES

A Tough Case to Crack

A Seed of Doubt

Roasted Peanuts and Peril

Chestnuts, Camping and Culprits

DONUT TRUCK COZY MYSTERIES

Deadly Deals and Donuts

Fatal Festive Donuts

Bunny Donuts and a Body

Strawberry Donuts and Scandal

Frosted Donuts and Fatal Falls

HEAVENLY HIGHLAND INN COZY MYSTERIES

Murdering the Roses

Dead in the Daisies

Killing the Carnations

Drowning the Daffodils

Suffocating the Sunflowers

Books, Bullets and Blooms

A Deadly Serious Gardening Contest

A Bridal Bouquet and a Body

Digging for Dirt

WENDY THE WEDDING PLANNER COZY MYSTERIES

Matrimony, Money and Murder

Chefs, Ceremonies and Crimes

Knives and Nuptials

Mice, Marriage and Murder